Hells Canyon

The Circuit Rider Series,
PART TWO

DENNIS ELLINGSON

Copyright © 2014 Dennis Ellingson.

All rights reserved. No part of this book may be used or reproduced by any means, graphic, electronic, or mechanical, including photocopying, recording, taping or by any information storage retrieval system without the written permission of the publisher except in the case of brief quotations embodied in critical articles and reviews.

All Bible quotations are from the K.J.V. of the era of the setting of this story.

WestBow Press books may be ordered through booksellers or by contacting:

WestBow Press
A Division of Thomas Nelson & Zondervan
1663 Liberty Drive
Bloomington, IN 47403
www.westbowpress.com
1 (866) 928-1240

Because of the dynamic nature of the Internet, any web addresses or links contained in this book may have changed since publication and may no longer be valid. The views expressed in this work are solely those of the author and do not necessarily reflect the views of the publisher, and the publisher hereby disclaims any responsibility for them.

Any people depicted in stock imagery provided by Thinkstock are models, and such images are being used for illustrative purposes only. Certain stock imagery © Thinkstock.

ISBN: 978-1-4908-2903-6 (sc)
ISBN: 978-1-4908-2904-3 (e)

Library of Congress Control Number: 2014904149

Printed in the United States of America.

WestBow Press rev. date: 03/18/2014

Contents

Introduction xi
Chapter 1 – At First Light 1
Chapter 2 – Trouble Anew 20
Chapter 3 – A Journey Considered 35
Chapter 4 – An Unexpected Journey 46
Chapter 5 – No Easy Time 61
Chapter 6 – Final Hours 84
Chapter 7 – The Little Ones 92
Chapter 8 – The Right Thing To Do 100
Chapter 9 – The Reckoning 112
Epilogue 125

"Blessed be God, even the Father of our Lord Jesus Christ, the Father of mercies, and the God of all comfort; Who comforteth us in all our tribulation, that we may be able to comfort them which are in any trouble, by the comfort where with we ourselves are comforted of God." 2nd Corinthians 1:3&4

Thanks, again, to my wife Kit for all her help with editing and providing the wonderful photographs that accompany this story.

Again I thank the Heavenly Father for seeing fit to have me live and roam the wonderful places of Oregon; East and West of the Cascades.

Introduction

Welcome to the second book in the Circuit Rider series. More than likely you have followed along with us learning about a man by the name of John Luke Mark Matthews or, as he likes to be called, J.L. You have discovered that he has begun to learn of the ways of the Lord through the help and words of a circuit rider. You also discovered that evil is everywhere and that one pursues Matthews, meaning to take his life. And you discovered The Dalles, the end of the Oregon Trail, and also a stunning wonder called The Painted Hills.

In this adventure we will travel to one of the greatest wonders of the world. This place is Hells Canyon, which is located on the Northern Oregon and Idaho borders. When my wife and I first beheld this wonder we could not take it all in, similar to how a visit to Grand Canyon in Arizona would affect you. This place is so big and so dramatic it is hard to get your thoughts and feelings around it. There is this interesting fact about Hells Canyon: while it might not be as grand as Grand Canyon and certainly not as visited as much, it does hold a distinction that Grand Canyon cannot claim. It is deeper. You can stand at the bottom like we did, aboard a boat in the middle of the Snake River and look up one full mile or more to see the top.

Hells Canyon is a wild and mysterious place. It is huge in scope and size. No matter how many visits you may make you will probably feel like we do, we have just barely scratched the surface on all this spectacular place is about.

Hells Canyon is the deepest gorge or canyon in North America, eclipsing Grand Canyon by thousands of feet. The reason for this is an impressive mountain range on the Idaho side known as the Seven Devils. Hells Canyon is so huge that it borders three Western States, Washington, Oregon and Idaho. Hells Canyon is the main course for the Snake River but many other rivers and creeks find their way to the bottom of this abyss.

Hells Canyon's origin is believed by scientists to have been created during a short catastrophic period known as the Missoula Flood. It can be believed and there is good evidence for this. There was a great lake located in what is now Montana, formed during the ice age that happened shortly after the worldwide flood of Noah. This lake was naturally dammed by ice, when that melted a tremendous amount of water was unleashed carving out canyons, gorges and other features in the process. This is how Hells Canyon was formed. From the creationist point of view Hells Canyon is new geology, less than 6000 years old.

Its name origin is shrouded in a bit of mystery. History seems to indicate the place was originally called Box Canyon, however that seems to be a name before the full length of it was seen and navigated. The name Hells Canyon seems to have its beginnings in, either peoples description of it as as a Hell on earth kind of a place, or what we discovered visiting it in August, way too hot! The stifling one hundred plus degrees during the days and temperatures that only cooled into the low eighties at night giving people the thought this was a bit of hell on earth.

None the less the canyon is a draw to both animal and humankind. There are abundant herds of mule deer and elk, ample amounts of bear, cougar and bobcat and, in the early days, large herds of Big Horn Sheep. Fishing the great Snake River is a wonder as well. I have never fished a river so full of fish. Today, this is somewhat different than it was before the three dams were created that hold great reservoirs. Salmon and Steelhead once had been much more abundant.

Natives have been coming for millenniums, their pictographs decorate the walls in many places and evidence of their camps can still be found.

The flora is abundant and diversified in places including what you would expect to see, Ponderosa Pine, Juniper and Sage, but also blackberries and many other kinds of wild fruit, flowers and cactus abound.

To this day in Hells Canyon there are still areas barely seen by man. The pioneers who traveled the Oregon Trail would have gotten their first glimpse of this awesome canyon at a place called Farewell Bend.

What must have God thought when he created this place? J.L. will discover more about God, himself and others as he finds himself lost but found in this awesome place.

Chapter One
At First Light

*"Even as I have seen, they that plow iniquity,
And sow wickedness, reap the same."*
Job 4:8

Reverend Gideon Thomas was dead and buried in the Painted Hills. His killer, the evil Clinton Jeffers was still on the loose. J.L. was at home with his wife Maddie and son Jacob. Spring was in full hilt. The wildflowers that covered the green hills of the Columbia Gorge were an awesome sight to behold. Maddie had picked Balsam Root, Lupine, Indian Paintbrush and other flowers, and displayed them in an old vase on the kitchen table. Their contrast of colors, yellows, purple and reds and blues added life to the darkening room.

Since J.L. had returned from the Painted Hills, it had been a night and a full day, and the next night was coming with the setting sun. J.L. was sitting at the table picking at a piece of pie and sipping the coffee, while vacantly looking at the vase of wildflowers on the table.

"It's quite a display this year John," Maddie stated. She wondered where her husband was in his thoughts.

"What'd ya say Maddie?" J.L. asked perking up and trying to focus his attention on his wife.

"Oh, nothing John, I was just talking about the wildflowers this year, it seemed like you were looking intently at that vase."

"Yep, mighty pretty this year," J.L. commented although his thoughts were far from there. "Maddie, I got to get over to Goldendale. I needed to make sure you two were fine and I certainly needed the rest and old Gus did too. But I got a job in front of me and I don't look forward to it."

"You say that Reverend Thomas' family is over there?"

"Yep, I am pretty sure that is what he told me. It seems there were sons and daughters if I recollect right. They need to know and it is my responsibility to fill them in."

"Did Gideon leave a widow then?" Maddie's curiosity about the family was growing.

"No, I am pretty sure he said that she had passed on some years back."

"I could come with you if that would be a help?" Maddie offered.

J.L. gave that a thought for a moment thinking a women's touch would be good but on second thought then stated, "Thanks, that would be helpful but I think this is something I need to do on my own."

"How far is Goldendale from here?" queried Maddie.

"It is on the Washington side, east and north of here. Probably a day's ride but I expect I would be gone overnight. I guess I would ride down to Biggs to catch the ferry and go on from there. I don't think it is a big town so it shouldn't be hard to find his family. But, I think I need to leave tomorrow, early, and try to be back the next day. I don't like to leave you alone but I will let the marshal know that I will be gone."

"I think I know how you are feeling. You are still shouldering the blame for something that falls to Clint Jeffers and him alone," Maddie tried to reassure.

"Maddie, I think that now and then, too. If it hadn't been for my wayward ways I think Gideon would be alive today. I guess I think the Lord has been hard pressed on me about all this so I can really understand how our ways affect things we don't even realize."

"Perhaps, John, but it doesn't change one bit that evil was done and not at your hand. I hate to see you take responsibility for something that is not yours to own."

"I guess I am still muddling it through but it doesn't change the fact that those poor people over there need to know about their father. And that is my job to do."

Maddie didn't know what else to say but rose and gave her a husband a hug. "I love you John. I love who you are becoming and yes, you need to go. It is the right thing to do and the sooner the better."

J.L. had a thought, as if a light went on for him. Rising from the table he went into the front room and retrieved the saddle bags of Gideon Thomas which were stowed in a corner. He felt as if he were snooping in a place he didn't need to be looking. It was his Bible that he was looking for. When he found it he brought it back to the table, sat down and opened the cover. He was correct in his hope. Listed there on the front page were the names of his family.

First mentioned was Gideon's name, date of birth and location.

Second, interestingly enough, was the name of a son, his name and birth place. He had been given the name of Joseph.

Then there was Martha, his wife, and then one daughter named Abigail, another son named Benjamin and one more daughter after that, she was named Hannah.

Reading on there was a number of names of grandchildren, which there were plenty.

This discovery now only motivated J.L more. Seeing these names made these people real and their need to know about their father.

* * *

At first light J.L. was up, making it a quick breakfast of coffee and biscuits before Maddie awoke. She walked out on the front porch sleepily, rubbing the sleep from her eyes, her auburn hair a wild snarl, J.L. had Gus out front and already saddled. Goliath was taking great interest of what was taking place and J.L. was thinking what would be best. Should he take the dog and see if the family wanted him or leave him? Jacob and the big dog had become fast friends, except as a bunk mate, with Goliath taking the lion's share of the little cot each night. J.L. thought perhaps he would leave the dog home, but make sure the family knew of it. But, evidently Goliath had already made up his mind and was not about to budge from next to the horse and be coaxed back into the house.

"I guess that answers it for me. Goliath will go and have the opportunity to be with the family. But, I know Jacob is already claimed him so I will make sure they know that he has a home with us if that would be alright," said J.L. to Maddie.

"I will be back before sundown tomorrow, and on my way, I will stop by the Marshal's office and let them know you and Jacob are alone," J.L. said moving closer to Maddie who had snuggled into his arms.

"We'll be fine, you do what needs to be done. I am going to pray for you, John," and with that Maddie began. "Lord, thanks again for bringing my husband home and in more ways than one. Thank-you Lord for what you are doing for him. Lord through this all we need to see your plan and just know how we ought to feel about all that has happened. I ask Thee to shed grace upon my husband and give him just the right words to say to Gideon's family that somehow this awful event can be some blessing for all." She then gave her husband a peck on the cheek, looked at him and decided that was not enough and kissed him full on the lips as a reminder of what he had back home.

* * *

As J.L. rode towards The Dalles, off to his left, the great Columbia River shimmered in the early morning light. For the moment the wind was mostly still and the water was lightly rippled in the new day. It looked like a river of shiny gems, heavenly perhaps. The hills, everywhere to be seen, on both banks, were as green as they would be during the year.

J.L didn't really remember what day it was, but concluded it was Friday and people were already out and in route to one place or another. Farmers were in the fields, women folk were out in the chicken coops or the gardens. School aged children were out and bound for school and probably thinking that school for the summer couldn't be soon enough, there were too many adventures to be had.

J.L. was thinking about the last few days and the turn of events in The Painted Hills. He had felt God's presence so much during those days with the circuit rider and he felt he had learned more about the ways of God. Then the terrible event and now he didn't know, he just simply didn't know.

He was grateful for the night and full day he'd had with his family and the fact that the relationship between them all was now well on the way to being patched up. Perhaps, at this point, that was the best part to concentrate on. He had lost much in the lunacy of his drinking and fighting ways. Now with a couple of months of sobriety he was able to see just how much he lost and how blessed he was to get it all back again. Maybe this was how God was working, because he didn't see it in the senseless death of that kind servant who had saved his life.

As he entered into town, there were a few saloons that he passed before getting to the marshal's office. He looked at them in a disdain he didn't think he would have ever felt. Yet, there was this sensation, this thought, like a tickling at the back of his mind, that said, 'Stop, have a few, it will do you good.' It was a like a chill went through him with that thought, voice, whatever, suggesting a drink or two or more. He shrugged into his coat a little more even though he really wasn't cold. Maddie had gotten it for him from old Mr. Larson, although the coat looked like it was old, it was hardly worn at all. He had brought it along to stave off the coming night if he were camping out. It could be a cold one especially if the wind might howl.

Could he really say he would never drink again? He thought he could and yet there was a little voice that said, 'Today you won't but what about tomorrow?' It was also at that moment that words from the Good Book that Gideon had shared came to mind and that had to do with something regarding that no temptation would befall him that was not something someone had before. Also that God would find away to overcome that temptation.

Now he had reached the marshal's office and although Marshal James was not there, Caleb was. He was sitting out on the boardwalk, yawning and probably finishing up a night shift.

"J.L., how are you? I heard you were back in town," he commented stifling the yawn.

"I am good and you look like you are ready for 40 winks."

Caleb nodded and yawned again and added, "Are you just stopping to say 'Hi' or is there something on your mind?' J.L. had been to the marshal's office the day before to share with him what had all taken place.

"Marshal James filled you in then?" J.L. asked and Caleb nodded back.

"Well, I just wanted you all to know that I am heading over to Goldendale to see if I can talk with Reverend Thomas' family and, uh, I was hoping you might just keep an eye out for Maddie's sake.

"No sooner said than done," Caleb answered back. "You go do what needs to be done; thanks for doing that and we'll be sure to check on the Missus and that good boy of yours. When do you expect to be back?"

"Tomorrow; no matter what." J.L. said firmly.

"Looks like you got company, isn't that Gideon's dog?"

"Yep it is. We've adopted him I guess or I should I say he has adopted us. The family needs to know that he is fine and can have him back if they want."

"Well, you be careful and we will keep an eye out for Jeffers."

J.L. waved a good-bye and headed out of town. He would need to travel some ten miles to reach the ferry site at Biggs. There were a number of ferries along the river and it was the only way to get across. At Biggs this would put him right in line to travel up to Goldendale which sat another ten miles up in the Gorge. He had only been there once but he didn't recall much of it.

He headed Gus out on a good pace, Goliath trotting right along. Traveling this route to the east brought him more views of the bluffs and hills. The farther one would travel the more the land would turn arid. He remembered this scene well as he, Maddie and baby Jacob made their way the last miles of the Oregon Trail. It seemed like a time to reflect. In many ways he felt a different man than the young buck in his twenties full of life and energy. Towards the end of the journey, Maddie had been very ill and rode most of the way in the back and taking care of the baby.

The time seemed to be full of promise and it wasn't too long until their life in the gorge had really gotten underway. He kept wondering to himself what it was exactly that had side-railed their family life together. It was like something that gnawed at him and even though their life was full and certainly busy just trying to make a go of it, but the drinking began. At first it was just a little and then more and more and never enough until the awful culmination with Jeffers.

Now he was consumed with how to undue what had been done. He recognized that was impossible but he seemed to feel the need to be making amends, making things right, setting the course straight, and yet the desire to drink was still there. At times his thinking would be a mix of thoughts that were such a contrast that he could hardly believe it was the same person thinking all of those thoughts.

He was pleased with himself that a new day had dawned. He had a sense that he saw the alcohol for what it really was; the enemy. It was just the arguing within himself to not lay down with the enemy ever again.

He recognized truly that God had moved in his life, the very fact that he was alive, healthy and on this mission spoke of something beyond his own abilities and desires. Yet there were so many unanswered questions about God and why the things in this life of joy and sorrow happened as they did. First and foremost was Gideon who had literally given his life for him. He suspected that he knew enough of Gideon to know that if the bullet that was to take his life was to be known about first he would not have changed a thing and have been the willing sacrifice.

J.L. doubted within himself that he could ever live up to the sacrifice; perhaps that was the way of it, no one has the ability to live up to what another is willing to give up.

As he rode along, the sun danced upon the river and the hills. Suddenly he noticed an unusual affect upon the water and sky, like a rainbow but more like a prism. Refracted light seemed to make the shape of a rough cross in front of him, like a rainbow colored cross. J.L. looked at intently, now oblivious to that which was around him. And then it struck him as if God spoke to him, 'This is sacrifice; that one who is not worthy would have one who would die for him anyway. It is what I did for you and for all that have lived, live now and will ever live. I give you undeserved love, my grace. I give you a love that comes from my heart and nothing from what you have done.'

He felt greatly moved within himself, as if in his very spirit right at the bottom of his heart. He was not sure how to explain it. It was not a thought or really even a feeling but something deeper than that. It was a joy of unsettling magnitude and he knew he would never forget the moment. But the moment didn't last for long.

In his trip, as dog, horse and man proceeded along, they would move in and out of rock bluffs, open areas and by small streams. At one time in full sun, which was quite warm, then in shady areas where it was actually hard to make out the trail because of the brightness of the sun a moment before.

It was in a shadowy spot when all of a sudden Goliath was barking wildly and Gus was beginning to back up and buck. It was all J.L. could do to stay mounted and yet try to see what was taking place in front of them in the shadows. Goliath was in front of the horse, nearly in the way and in danger of being trampled but Gus was trying to back up and bucking and in the midst of the noise J.L. could hear a noise that was not uncommon to him, the sound of a rattling and a hissing. Then as Gus moved to the side a bit he could see one of the largest Western Diamond Back Rattlers he had ever seen. Goliath was pawing at it and the snake was trying to strike him, Gus and anything else that seemed a threat.

J.L. leapt from the horse and at the same time pulling his 30-30 from the scabbard. Once on the ground he fired a shot. Not so much hoping to strike the snake but to get Goliath and Gus startled enough to move away. The tactic worked but now the striking, angry snake's focus of attention and fangs was near on to J.L. So close was the venomous serpent that J.L. could feel the air move as he struck out. In fact the snake was so close he could not get a shot off but instead clumsily bat at the snake with the barrel of the gun. That tactic, however, was sufficient to move it away and in the next instant J.L. raised the gun, aimed fast and fired. The first shot hit the snake about mid-body which stopped it then with another second to think and aim the second shot hit him in the head stopping the onslaught.

Gus was still shimming away but now settling down and Goliath moved close to inspect the intruder. J.L. reached down grabbed the carcass and flung it as far as he could but it was also at that moment, like being hit by brilliant light or perhaps more of a sudden sense of evil, that he realized that there was an enemy that was not just the serpent or just Clinton Jeffers but an invisible one who wanted not just him but anyone and everyone else in the world down, suffering, dead and gone to hell.

Goliath trotted back as if to say, 'I did a good job getting your attention' and J.L. reciprocated by petting the big dog's head. Gus now stood quietly waiting for his master to approach him and soon the three were off again no worse for the experience and J.L. now more mindful of the spiritual side of things that evil exists and there is one ultimately responsible for it. He knew he would need to give it more thought.

By mid-morning the three reached the ferry dock. It wasn't much, a wooden pier and a little hut. The ferry, J.L. noticed, was on its way back across the river about half way. He dismounted Gus and wandered on to the pier. A young woman, no more out of her teens, J.L. estimated, hollered out. "Mr. are you alookin' to cross today?"

"Yes Ma'am." J.L. answered back.

"It won't be but a bit and my Pa will take you directly as soon as he crosses. It'll cost you four bits."

"That sounds good to me. It's a fair price for a boat ride if you ask me." J.L. answered back.

The girl was friendly with a buck toothed smile and a tomboy way about her. "My name's Sara." Said the girl extending a thin hand to shake J.L.'s but at the same time looking at Goliath like he might be familiar to her.

"Nice to meet you, Ma'am" said J.L. generously shaking her hand in his big paw.

"Ain't nobody called me Ma'am before." she said, still smiling that toothy grin.

"Well then it was my pleasure."

The girl looked like she was about to say something else but didn't get the chance.

"Sari", a voice called out from the ferry, "Get ready to catch the lines!"

"Comin' Pa" she answered back and got busy about securing the lines forward and aft of the small ferry. There were just a couple of people aboard, with horses, getting ready to make their departure

The Ferry captain was a wiry man middle aged and it was obvious where Sara got her looks.

Once the other's had departed J.L. coaxed Gus on, who wasn't so sure he thought it was a good idea. Goliath trotted right on and went up to greet the Captain.

"Hey, I know this big ole boy. Is that you Goliath?" J.L. answered for the dog. "Yes sir, that would be him."

The captain seemed a little puzzled and looked around expecting to see another. "Where is the preacher man?" Evidently he had crossed the river here enough times to make the Captain's acquaintance.

J.L. realized that it was going to be his task, telling strangers to himself about Gideon's passing.

J.L. approached the man, extended a hand. "My name is J.L. and I am on my way over to Goldendale to talk with Gideon's family and to tell them what I have to tell you today. I am sorry to say it, Gideon is dead."

"Lord have mercy!" said the stunned man obviously moved by what he heard. "Sari", hollered the captain to his daughter who was now walking back to the hut. "Come here a sec."

Soon the girl was on board. "Would you tell her what you just told me?" J.L. obliged and filled in, in brief, the circumstances of Gideon's passing.

"I am as sorry to hear that as anything there is." The captain commented. "We talked quite a bit and he took a real interest in Sara. He got her, her first bible."

"I know that he touched many lives and he saved mine twice", said J.L.

Now there was a sense of outrage in the captain's voice. "What's being done about this fella, what'd you say his name was?"

"Jeffers, Clint Jeffers and yes the marshal in The Dalles is doing what he can to catch him."

Sara's smile was gone and she was quiet as she stepped back off the boat. She set the lines free, the captain pulled them in and they were off to the other side, J.L., horse and dog his only customers for this trip.

J.L. thought he might talk more with the boat captain more but the winds on the river were keeping him busy so J.L. just took in the short trip across. He had only been across the Washington side a couple of times and never at this point so he enjoyed the view of the gorge from the middle of the great river. Looking west he could see enough of a distance to see the land change in color, darker green indicating the great forests that lie on the rainy side of the Cascades. To look east revealed the still green hills but a land that became more arid with every mile. The contrast was great. Somehow he imagined the clouds getting stuck on the mountains until enough of their water was let loose for them to travel east or dissipate altogether.

As he arrived on the Washington side, he took pleasure in seeing his homeland from the distance and marveled at the step of the hills and mountains that would rise to the great snowy heights of Mt. Hood, Mt. Jefferson and others. He had heard about the Three Sisters, great mountains in Central Oregon named from the bible, they were Faith, Hope and Charity.

As the boat pulled in, a young man greeted them and was there to tend to the lines. He was the spitting image of his dad and sister and it turned out that this boy, named Samuel, was Sara's twin brother.

The Captain took a few moments, as there being no customers on the Washington side, to talk with J.L. and introduce his son. Again he left the responsibility for J.L. to share about what had happened to Gideon. Samuel was troubled as well but made a curious response. "He was a good old guy, but see Pa, what good did all that preachin' do him?"

The father's face began to turn red and J.L. wondered what kind of response there might have been if he had not been there rather than the captain just stating, "You watch your mouth, boy, you should have some respect for your elders and one as kind as the Reverend was. He gave you your first bible too, just like your sis. The difference is she has read it and yours looks as new as the day you got it." The captain began to look at J.L. as if hoping he would say something in Gideon's defense. And J.L. knew he should, but wasn't sure what to say. Then it came to him, just what he had been thinking about earlier.

"Son, I don't know as much about the Good Book as I should and I sure would have liked to have gotten to know the preacher better. But I know this about him. He did not do that preaching for himself. Not one bit. He did it for others and maybe it's not been any good for you but I can tell you now, I am alive because that man believed The Word and gave his life for God. And somewhere in that book and maybe I should know better it says something like *"For whosoever will save his life shall lose it; but whosoever shall lose his life for my sake and the gospel's, the same shall save it."*

"Mr. did he tell you that?" the boy asked.

"No, he did not tell me that, but he read it to me during the times we were together. And if it hadn't been for your words I may have not remembered that. I think if ole Gideon were able to step out of heaven today and answer your question he would tell you that he sought nothing but to serve and gained everything because of it."

"Thank you very much, J.L. I think those were just the words this foolish boy needed to hear." said the captain.

J.L. took a few more minutes to enquire of Gideon's family, if the captain knew them. It turns out that he did and told J.L. where he might find the son named Benjamin. It was the same name that he had seen in Gideon's old bible.

J.L. turned Gus' head and found the rough road that climbed up and out of the gorge heading to Goldendale. It was a few more miles, ranches and farms lined the road, growing more populated as J.L. approached the town. Goldendale sat up on the bluff overlooking the gorge. Its main street was lined with stores, saloons and some public buildings. J.L. looked for Thomas' Mercantile, the store the siblings owned together. It was managed by the sister and her husband. When he found the store he noticed there was much merchandise set out upon the boardwalk. He tied Gus to the hitching post and entered the store. Compared to the bright day, the store was dim of light but he spotted a tall angular figure of a woman standing behind a counter.

She boomed out, "Mister, welcome to our store, I don't believe I've made your acquaintance." The voice was distinctly feminine, medium in range and familiar to him. Abigail or Hannah, he assumed, had the tone and timbre of Gideon's voice.

"No Ma'am, you have not. I come from over the river, The Dalles."

"Sir, I am Abigail", she said while extending a hand. J.L. gripped it and was surprised at the strength in her long fingers. He gauged her to be in her fifties, handsome and pale in appearance.

"Yes, Ma'am that is what I believed it would be"

"Pardon me; are you specifically looking for me?"

"Truth be known, exactly you, your sister and your brother or, uh, brothers?" J.L. began to stammer, then catching himself, "I am J.L. Matthews and I am on a mission to speak to you . . . it is about your father, Gideon Thomas . . . uh, that is correct, right?"

"Yes, Reverend Thomas is my father . . ." she seemed to want to continue but was not sure what to say next.

J.L. thought for a moment, almost too quickly he was now in front of an offspring of Gideon's and he wished beyond measure that he had better news.

"Mr.?" Abigail asked with a bit of apprehension in her voice and the appearance on her face to go with it.

"Ma'am, I can't tell you how much I hate to tell you this, but I bring sad news, your wonderful father has gone on to meet his maker."

"What is this? Are you saying my father has died?" Abigail said, her voice rising and her hand as well to her face. "Oh, I knew this would eventually happen." She said almost to herself. She then looked J.L. squarely in the face and with a voice almost too calm asked. "How did this happen, how did my father die?"

"Well, Ma'am, I am fine to tell you, it is a bit of a story. Is it possible to tell the others as well, at the same time?"

"Oh . . . well certainly." said Abigail straightening herself. I am just going to close the store, nearly time anyway. I will take the buggy, pick up my sister, Hannah, she lives here in town and then you can follow me out to the ranch that my brother Benjamin has." She seemed to be planning her next move as she explained.

"And your brother, Joseph, is he about?"

"No he is not." She said matter of fact and offering nothing else.

Soon the store was closed, Abigail in a surrey and J.L. following along. They went a short distance to a nicely kept house just a few blocks downtown. There he met Hannah whom was about the opposite of appearance than Abigail. She was of fuller figure and much shorter. He also met her husband. Soon they were in the surrey and now headed out of town, to the north for the fifteen minute ride to the ranch that was Benjamin's.

Upon arrival J.L. noted that it was a sprawling affair of one large house and many barns and out buildings. A substantial head of cattle grazed in the distance.

Benjamin or Ben, as he preferred, was the spittin' image of his father only younger. His wife was there too, along with a couple of ranch hands who were of Hispanic descent, J.L. guessed.

Soon the three siblings, with two spouses, were gathered in the spacious, well appointed parlor. All were quiet, sitting and waiting.

J.L. tried to sit too and wished Maddie was here. He stood, changed his mind and then sat on the edge of a chair.

Hannah stated, "It's alright, J.L. we are not surprised to learn of our father's passing. He was getting too old for the circuit although you could not tell him that."

J.L. started, "Your father was a brave man, saved my life twice and I am here because he isn't." Quickly but thoroughly J.L. told the story first of Gideon being shot and killed in The Painted Hills by a man name Clint Jeffers then retracing he told the whole of the story about being himself being found by Goliath a month before, the chance meeting on the trail and so on.

This created a lot of questions; 'where is Father buried, where is the Painted Hills, how do we get there? What about this Clint Jeffers, any chance that he could be brought to justice soon?'

J.L., himself, had a burning question, part of it he could only state at the moment. "Where is your brother, Joseph, I feel a real need to let him know too."

This was followed by a moment of quiet discomfort. Finally Ben spoke up. "We are not sure but we believe somewhere along the Snake River in Oregon or Idaho. A place called Box Canyon."

"Box Canyon?" J.L. asked, "I don't think I know the place."

"It is also called Hells Canyon. It is that area on the Snake beyond Farewell Bend near Ontario."

"That I know, or at least know of."

J.L. and some others, years ago now, when coming across in the wagon train, had gone out a day's distance to hunt for game. The canyon he saw was beyond description, huge, deep and wild.

Anticipating his question, "They have discovered mineral there, gold and silver. Joseph has gone on to stake his claim. He left about a year ago and we haven't heard from him since."

J.L. squirmed; his sense of duty prodded and questioned him, do I need to seek him out?

"I guess it is high time we found out how our brother Joseph is doing and take him the news." stated Ben. "I will set out before the end of the week." There was a determination in his voice. This did not deter the flood of dissent from the two sisters.

"I am trying to be polite in front of our guest," started Abigail, "but I don't think Joe could give a hoot if Father is dead. He will find out soon enough, when and if he returns."

There was obviously some animosity here amongst the siblings.

Hannah spoke up, more quiet and deferring but with no less the same thought. "It will do no good for you to go that distance. He will not much care, I fear."

Hannah's husband, Pete, came to the defense of the sisters, "Think about how far that is, it would take you a month and nothing less if you could find him. This is a busy time to be away from the ranch. I say let him find out when he comes back."

"I appreciate what you are saying, in fact, I agree. But it doesn't change our duty to Father and not Joseph," said a resolute Ben.

J.L. was trying to figure out how to shrink his large frame into the woodwork so to be unnoticed.

Everyone, at once, seemed to notice his discomfort. "Sorry, J.L. this is a family affair, and you have done what is needed," stated Ben. "We can't thank you enough for coming over here to tell us about our father."

Abigail then said, "If, in any way you are feeling guilty about this please put your heart to rest. This is what my father lived his life for, to see others find their way with Christ. In his way of thinking this was what life was about. He taught us well, we knew that his life was a sacrifice so to find out he died as a sacrifice is not a loss for us."

"You may not understand this fully now," Hannah chimed in, "but father would have had it no other way."

Pete stated with some emotion in his voice, "He died with his boots on."

J.L. was silent for a bit then said, "Thank you, I appreciate your kind words and it gives me much to think about. The day is getting late, and if I hope to get back to the other side I need to leave."

Ben's wife Lois stated, "It is too late for you to get the ferry by now, J.L., please stay with us tonight. It will give us more time to talk. You can leave rested in the morning. We would like the pleasure of your company for awhile longer." stated Abigail. There were nods and murmurs indicating that all agreed in unison.

It turned out to be a fine evening. A sumptuous meal was served, which J.L. relished. There was conversation about Gideon and his exploits.

One such story as told by the three siblings really caught J.L.'s attention, not to mention tickling his funny bone.

Seems there was a time when Gideon and Martha took in a stranger. A homely little man that everyone, including himself, called Ogre, like the fairy tale creatures that scared people as they crossed bridges.

Ogre was one of these chaps that just never seemed to get a break. He had grown up back east. As a kid he was bounced around from relatives to orphanages because his father had run out and his mother had died young. But by fourteen he was on his own. He also liked the liquor so when he had some money in his pocket it was soon spent on that.

He had never had a place to call his home except for a stint in the militia and an occasional jail when he got into minor trouble for being drunk or a vagrant. He didn't seem to be real adept at much but if he was working he tried his best. No one of the fairer sex ever gave him much more than the time of day so he had been a bachelor all his days.

He managed to get west hitching on with a wagon train and helping out the wagon master by taking care of the stock animals. But once out west his horizons didn't seem to broaden much and he lived a pretty meager existence.

One day he found his way to the Reverend's door. Gideon was away on another circuit ride. At home were Mrs. Thomas and the three kids. The oldest, Joseph, was already of age and had moved out.

It was getting to be late in the summer. The work seemed to be piling up although the kids did what they could. Gideon was delayed and Mrs. Thomas had her hands full. What would have normally been an invite to supper for Ogre turned out to be an opportunity to sleep in the barn and help out for a week for food, board and earn a few dollars.

As homely and rough around the edges as Ogre was, the family found there was just something endearing about him. And after Gideon returned, he and Martha set out to try to rehabilitate Ogre and change his wandering ways.

"Nah, folks, youse been kind enough and I thank you for what you done but I got to get to going," Ogre said trying to bow out gracefully. Seems his itinerant years had given him a pair of itchy feet and he was never happy to settle in one place for too long.

"But winter is coming on" appealed Gideon. "And this can be harsh country in the winter."

"Well, I'm a headin' south, I dunno maybe Frisco or beyond."

"That is too far to go now, you will never make it, and you have no horse." Mrs. Thomas pleaded.

"Well, maybe ifin I'm lucky I will catch a ride with a mule skinner headin' south."

"Ogre, I mean Sir" said Gideon, who despised calling the little man that, "pardon me for saying it but you are a pretty sore sight and I don't know if you could get a ride. Stay with us through the winter, then come spring, if you want to go you will have a little money, you will be all cleaned up because my Mrs. will see to that. Fresh duds, my son, you will have a running chance of getting south."

Ogre scratched his unshaven chin and scratched what was left of the hair on his head.

"We'll even get a room built for you in the barn and put a real bed there." Mrs. Thomas promised, giving her husband a sideward glance as he tried to replace the surprised look on his face at this task he was now facing with an appearance that looked like he was in complete agreement.

"No strings attached, come spring, better clothes, at least $20 in your pocket and a few baths, why anyone would like you along for a ride south."

This appealed to Ogre and he soon agreed. And he became a part of the family. He liked tinkering, found things to fix and enjoyed doing it. The family discovered that he had nearly no education at all and could not read. So when there was family reading time in the evening Ogre was invited to join in and even encouraged to give reading a try. He did try but it was apparent by the look on his face it was he was embarrassed by not knowing much of readin', writin' and 'rithmetic.

Often in the late afternoon or when he was catching a breath of fresh air, Ogre was seen staring off down the road to parts unknown. After one particularly nice and warm fall day Ogre announced to Mrs. Thomas that he needed to get going. He appreciated their kindness so much but he thought he would take advantage of the nicer weather and head south to 'Frisco.

When Gideon returned home later and Mrs. Thomas told him of Ogre's decision to leave, he was right out to confront and try to convince Ogre to think different. But no matter of protest or lecture was working after an hour of discussion.

Finally Gideon said, "Well, this is what I am going to do if you decide in the morning to do this hair-brained idea of yours. I am going to pray that you will not be seen, uh, like invisible. That the wagons and such passing by on the main road just won't see you as you try to bargain a ride."

Gideon could tell that Ogre could barely keep a straight face but was working hard to be respectful. Good-byes were said and soon everyone had turned in.

Early the next morning as everyone rose, Mrs. Thomas was busy getting the children ready for school nobody really took notice if Ogre was around or not.

As Gideon headed out to do some rounds he checked in the barn and found Ogre's make-shift room empty and neatly straightened. That reminded him of the prayer he would pray, Lord, make this little man invisible, hide him in your hand so as not to be seen. Please, Lord, we would like to finish our work for you with him."

The day came and went quickly as most days seem to. The family was gathered for dinner. Their usual houseguest this last month or so was not present and they felt his absence.

"Pa", said "Abigail, did Ogre really leave?" She was usually first to ask questions because of her curiosity. "Do you think he will make it to Frisco?"

Just as Gideon was about to give her a long answer about life and things there came a loud rapping at the front door. "Hallo the house!" boomed a familiar voice. "Are youse all at home?"

William jumped up and ran to the front door and soon ushered in a most humble looking Ogre, albeit a bit tired.

"Looky who's here, it's Ogre!"

He was soon invited to the table, tore in to dinner as if there was no tomorrow and between bites explained that he waited out on the road no less than 10 hours and couldn't get a ride even a short distance.

Gideon and Mrs. Thomas had a smile playing on their faces. And when Ogre said, "Why it was like I was invisible." the two could contain themselves any longer and broke out in raucous laughter for a reverend and his wife.

J.L. could hardly wait to ask, "So what ever happened to Ogre."

"Oh you mean Mr. Schmidt? Why, he has worked at the hotel in town for 30 plus years. No one calls him Ogre anymore, just Mr.

Schmidt", piped in Abigail. Then adding, "I see him nearly every day. He reminds me that the power of prayer is not to be taken lightly."

The family was curious and attentive as J.L told about Maddie and himself and how they came to Oregon and how now they were working hard to fix the rough life they had lived in recent years because of J.L.'s drinking.

Later J.L. was ushered into a guest bedroom that was well appointed with the most comfortable bed he thought he had ever slept in. He wished he could share the experience with Maddie. As he drifted off to sleep he felt blessed and comfortable and in ways that he did not expect. Rather Goliath was happy to share it with him.

As he nodded off to sleep there was that one unanswered question that bothered him. He didn't know how to ask without seeming like he was sticking his nose into someone else's business. But it was obvious that there was animosity between these three siblings and the absent Joseph. He wondered if it could have anything to do with the entry in the bible – Gideon first, then Joseph, then Martha and then the rest of the children.

As much as he would like to know, it wasn't his business to ask, so for now he would try to let it be.

Chapter Two
Trouble Anew

"Many are the plans in a man's heart, but it is the Lord's purpose that prevails."
Proverbs 19:21

As comfortable as that bed was and as much as he would have liked to tarry, J.L. forced himself up early with the hopes of setting out before Ben and his wife were up. Before stepping out of the room though, the inviting aroma of coffee and breakfast cooking tickled at his nose. In the hallway J.L. was greeted by Ben who was coming from their inside commode or water closet as he had heard such a room called.

"Hungry? I am. Breakfast is about ready. You will need a good one for your long ride home" Ben said, extending his arm in invitation to the kitchen.

Lois was busy, clad in a colorful apron and humming some unrecognizable tune. "Good morning, J.L., hope you slept well." she said, smiling warmly at him. "And how about Goliath?" she added.

"Like a log ma'am, just not as quiet" J.L said with a little chuckle.

Soon the three of them were settled around a small kitchen table. Grace was said and the eating had commenced. Goliath got his fair share as well but out on the back porch.

"J.L.", Ben began, "We are planning a memorial service for father in a couple of weeks, probably two Saturdays from now. We sure would like you to attend. If you wouldn't mind, people would probably like to hear from you about his last days."

"Um, I believe I could do that." He said, wishing somehow he could have gulped down those words before he said them.

"Maddie and your son could come too. You would be our guests here." Spoke up Lois.

"Yes, I am sure Maddie would be honored. Uh, I am not much for speaking in front of groups of people but . . ."

"You just tell the story and share your heart, J.L. that is all anyone would hope for" Ben said matter-of-factly as if the matter was settled.

After breakfast J.L. was busy with getting Gus saddled. He had enjoyed a night in warm barn and plenty of oats he suspected. Goliath was hanging close, watching J.L. with great interest. This was a realization that the subject of the dog's place in this hadn't been discussed. 'He should stay here', J.L. thought, that is if they want him.

It was like Ben was reading his thoughts. "Has ole Goliath taken to that boy of yours and to Maddie? I reckon he has" he said, answering his own question.

"Well, yeah, seems that way but Goliath is rightly yours or your family's . . ." J.L started.

"Nonsense, I suspect that big dog has already made that decision and I don't think you would ride out of here without him wanting to come along."

As J.L. mounted his horse, after saying good bye to Ben, shaking his hand hard and after a hug from Lois, who insisted, he turned to head out. In that bright morning, the sun was warming the day up quickly, a gentle breeze played in his ears. But something crept up the back of J.L.s neck that made him stop. He started to turn to look back, to give a wave when, once again, a familiar and horrible sound broke the peace of the morning.

It was the sound of a thump, the sound of discharge of a heavy rifle and a groan coming from Ben who was now on the ground, holding his leg. Lois, too, had hit the ground, crawling towards her wounded husband. In a flash, J.L. with rifle grabbed from the scabbard in hand he was off the horse. To the distant south, near some oaks and firs, he caught sight of the familiar hat and coat of a man darting for cover. He lifted and fired off three shots in quick succession. They were not returned. Now running, he headed for the spot he had fired toward. He was stopped by barbwire but in that instant he saw horse and rider, some hundred yards away, making their retreat. He knew who it was. He emptied his carbine towards the target but to no avail. Clint Jeffers had once again done evil and had gotten away.

Quickly he ran back to Ben and Lois. By now Lois had shredded her colorful apron and had tied a tourniquet around Ben's right leg, above the knee. The knee was bloodied and shattered and Ben grimaced and moaned in pain.

"J.L., quick please, the doctor lives less than a mile down the road, look for the name, Jackson, on a signboard next to a white house," Lois said with anguish in her voice.

Back on Gus, J.L. made the quick trip, found the doctor just heading out for the morning, climbing into a surrey.

Within a matter of minutes they returned. Hoisted Ben to a sofa in the house and the doctor was busy.

"There is no slug to remove, seems as if it glanced off your knee but not without doing some damage that is going to keep you off your feet for a month at least. We don't need the tourniquet, loss of blood is minimal and no artery was hit. But good thinking Lois."

~~~

The matter was decided and J.L. had more money in his pocket than he had for a long time. In fact only one other time when he sold his parents farm, split the money with his brother and sisters and bought wagon and rig to head for Oregon.

It was now afternoon and he was headed back to Oregon and in time enough to get home before dark. It remained a brilliant day and quite warm. Warm enough so as to raise perspiration on the back of his neck and between his shoulder blades. He was giving the weather little thought though.

Goliath trotted alongside Gus, large tongue lolling has he moved. There was much to think about and much to tell Maddie and Jacob. Some of this he knew she wasn't going to be real happy with. He hoped her kind nature would over ride her feelings.

As he ruminated J.L. kept an eye out and the carbine was loaded and as much as he didn't like to do it, the safety was off. At the same time, he doubted that he would see Jeffers today. This gave thought to this bad man and why he was so intent on settling this score. Was there something more than just revenge? He couldn't imagine. He was also amazed at what a lousy shot he was. 'Must be that bum hand' he thought, otherwise he would have been dead to rights with a stationary target and that big gun.

He also wondered about God in all this. One thought just seemed to lead to another. The Thomas family was quick to give praise to God that J.L.'s life and Ben's life had been spared. But if Jeffers was such a lousy shot with that bum hand then why didn't God just deflect that a little bit more so that the shot missed altogether and Ben wasn't saddled with a shot up knee? These are things he did not understand about God's will, perfect will and the things of life that affected good and bad people alike and how, if at all, affected God. He knew he should get the bible out and read it for a better understanding. Maybe a visit with the pastor from the church would be a good idea. He sure wished he could talk with Gideon about this.

When J.L. thought of all that money now in his shirt pocket he wondered if what he had agreed to, even suggested, was indeed the right thing to do. Had he jumped to a decision based upon his own guilt and sense of responsibility? With this, he now recalled the conversation just before he left.

Ben had lay in his bed, groaning a bit but saying that he wasn't in too much in pain. Abigail was there; she was standing and pacing a bit. Hannah too was there and her husband. Lois sat by Ben's side.

"I can't begin to tell you how bad I feel about this" began J.L. "it seems my wayward life is having a terrible effect upon your lives, something you don't deserve. First it's your fine father and now, Ben."

Abigail approached Ben, putting her hand upon his arm. "Listen, we have to accept the way things are and just do the best with them."

"Well, that is what I want to do. But what is the best thing to do about this? That's why I came here. I couldn't imagine that Jeffers would follow me. You needed to know about your father and I could only see doing that in person," J.L. lamented.

"And you did do the right thing, it was honorable." said Lois.

"And God will honor this too." Ben stated through the pain.

J.L. wondered about that, how would God honor such a thing and this event that had taken place didn't seem to be any fine example of it.

"Well, folks, it doesn't change anything for me and that was to make sure the sons and daughters of Gideon knew of his brave passing. Now with you laid up, Ben, then I need to see if I can find Joseph out there in that Hell's Canyon," stated J.L. It felt like evil itself had paid a visit that day.

This sparked off a similar but short conversation, quickly subdued by Ben. Similar as before, about just how necessary it was to do this when some thought that if Joseph needed to know then when he returned would be soon enough.

"I for one don't think you have to go. I do believe that we do need to let Joseph know and maybe it is a month or so out but I still can plan to go," Said Ben.

This statement was greeted by the two sisters with disapproval again which Ben hushed with the wave of his hand.

Once again J.L. started, "Well, folks, I think I need to do this. I appreciate you letting me off the hook on this one and maybe I am just being stubborn but I think I will need to do this. I won't rest until I do."

The room was quiet for a moment. Abigail was first to speak, she was still pacing. There was more on her mind than just this. "Ben, Hannah" she started, "do you think we can use some of the funds for the ministry to take care of J.L.'s expenses if he is going to be mule stubborn about this?"

"I do not see why not" said Ben. "In my trip I was planning on stopping at the half dozen or so places that Father ministered in to let those good people know. Perhaps, J.L. if you insist, we could ask you to do that too? It would not greatly add to your trip in time. We have a record of who he visits."

"Yes, you would represent Father, his ministry and us by doing so. And this would only be fair. The bible is clear, 'a man is worth his wages'. You would be doing the Lord's work and honoring the name of Reverend Thomas as well," stated Abigail.

J.L.'s first thought was to decline the offer. He certainly did not feel like he was doing the Lord's work but rather an unwitting player in the devil's hand. He didn't even get a chance to say no.

"Good, that is settled. You do us a great favor. You can speak more clearly to the people about Dad's last days and in a way that I can't really explain at this point, you finding Joseph might be better than Ben. It might go easier." It was obvious that Abigail was use to making decisions in the family.

J.L wondered about that but at the same time was watching and listening as Abigail beckoned him to follow her to town, to the bank, to get his payment.

~~~

J.L. waited outside the bank, sitting on a step. Goliath, after drinking from a trough, decided that a good petting was in order and rested his huge head in J.L.'s lap.

In a few moments out came Abigail, envelope in hand which she immediately handed to J.L. "This, kind sir, is our way of saying thanks and wanting to help you make it easier to help us." She gave him a hug, patted Goliath and strode off down to her store.

Now, riding along J.L was pretty much oblivious to his surroundings and others on the road around him. The ferry was to capacity with folks traveling from one side to another. His plan was to leave the envelope in his shirt pocket until he got home but it seemed to weigh heavy and was bothersome. He waited until he was off the ferry, in a place by himself, and then pulled the envelope out of his pocket. He opened it and was surprised to see the amount of cash that was in there. There was also a little note, hastily written. "J.L., we wanted to make sure that this trip you will take for us is as little a burden as possible. Hopefully this will allow you to have the needed funds for your long travel and to help take care of things back home as well."

J.L. said aloud to the only ones around, Gus and Goliath, "Yes, fine lady and some . . . and some." That was followed by a long whistle which Goliath regarded with a cocked head of bewilderment.

Once in The Dalles J.L. headed directly to the Marshal's office. He didn't find Marshal James but his deputy Caleb was there.

"J.L. how was the trip? Come on in for a cup of coffee. It is so quiet today in town I'm afraid I might nod off." Caleb said.

That was an offer J.L. could not turn down, a little pick me up was needed.

"What brings you in today? Are you just back from Goldendale?"

"Yes," J.L. started.

"And did you have some luck with that?"

"Sure did, met one of his sons and the two daughters, spent the night out at the ranch. They were most hospitable and kindly in light of what took place."

"Well, that is good."

"Yeah, but that wasn't all", J.L. then went on to explain about the events of this morning and that he believed it was Jeffers who had fired the shot meant for him but wounding the son.

"Well, if that doesn't just beat all!" Caleb exclaimed. "What is with that hombre?" he said shaking his head. He thought for a minute then slammed a heavy fist down. "You don't worry. I will let Marshal James know tonight. We are going to do everything we can to find this devil."

~~~

The sun was low in the sky when he road into the yard of his home along the Chenoweth Creek. Jacob and Maddie were sitting out on the makeshift porch in old wooden chairs that he had fashioned years ago.

"Pa!" hollered Jacob who came running. When close enough he jumped up towards J.L. who caught him and hoisted him, giving him an awkward hug and a quick scrape with his beard on the boy's smooth face.

"How's my favorite son?"

"Good, Pa, but you need a shave."

Both of them were then off the horse and Maddie was in his arms and with a quick kiss.

"Oh, I missed you. Are you hungry?"

"Oh yeah, and I was only gone a day."

"Well, it seems longer than that. C'mon dinner is ready now and we don't want to let it wait any longer."

J.L. stopped to wash the dust off from the day and kicked off his boots. Jacob, without having to be asked, took care of Gus. Goliath would wait impatiently under the table waiting for his portion of dinner.

As the sun set the family gathered again, hands grasped by each other and Maddie prayed. "Lord, I thank you for bringing my husband back home safe and that we are altogether. Thank you for always watching out for us and in ways we may not even realize."

Dinner, as usual, was great and plentiful. He wondered sometimes how Maddie managed, they weren't poor by some standards but they sure weren't rich either.

J.L. decided to share that latter part of his journey with Maddie later. In the meantime he told them of Goldendale, Gideon's family, the folks that operated the ferry. Quietly, almost reverently he told them of the phenomena of the rainbow cross and then, shortly after that, the incident with the rattlesnake.

Because dinner was late, before Jacob wished it, it was his bedtime. Both Maddie and J.L. could hardly keep from yawing and shortly after that they were snuggled in their own bed.

"John, I get the feeling there was more to what happened that you said," started Maddie quietly.

Without saying a word, J.L. got back up and took the envelope that Abigail had given him and handed it to Maddie. "Take a look, and then I will tell you the rest."

Maddie opened it, looked at J.L., closed it, looked at J.L. again and this time pulled the wad from the envelope and counted it.

"John, do you realize how much is here?"

"Nope but quite a bit more than I am used to seeing."

"We could live on this for . . . for some time to come!" Maddie stuttered.

"Well, Maddie, that is the idea."

J.L. then told her the rest of what had taken place, the shooting, him spotting who he believed to be Clint Jeffers, his volunteering to go to Hells Canyon and the family promising to make his time financially worthwhile.

"Maddie, I also said that you would have to be alright with this too. I have no problem in sending this money right back."

"John," was all Maddie wanted to say for the night. She blew the lamp out on the bedside, rolled over away from him, although still with her backside pressed up to him.

"You want to wait till morning to talk about this?" he asked but it was more a statement that he knew would not be answered tonight.

She nodded her head and said no more than, "Uh huh."

J.L. thought he would surely not sleep a wink tonight but the weariness of the trip overtook him and he was soon out. On the other hand Maddie would tarry in her thoughts for some while. She didn't really know what she thought. She did know how she felt and that was elation and sadness, almost anger.

The money was like a gift from heaven unexpected, and how they could use it, like manna only in greenbacks. But the thought of her husband away for at least a good month, maybe more, was not something she looked forward to at all. Not this year especially. Here he was sober, had found the Lord and they were more of a family than they had ever been. The future was promising and the things they could do this year to grow the ranch were better than ever. Her Christian sense about this said she was being selfish and that he was needed, perhaps even by the Good Lord himself, to go to this far away place. John said it was called something like Hells Canyon. She remembered Farewell Bend and the foreboding canyon that stretched north from there when they stayed for a few days before moving on in the wagon train.

What would it be like to try to track one human being in that incredible wilderness? What dangers lay ahead? What was in that place that few white men even knew about?

For too long she realized that she had mulled this over and had not given it over to God. And so she prayed, long, hard but in quietness. She thanked God and yet she poured her heart out too. She didn't feel like there was an answer, yet there was a sense of peace, a little like standing in a safe place in the midst of a storm. There it was all around you, yet if you remained where you were you were windblown a bit but safe. Finally sleep came and daylight about a minute after that she thought.

~~~

It was Sunday and as a family they had not been to church since J.L. had left for the cattle drive a month ago. As tired as Maddie was, she rousted her men, got busy in the kitchen, with the laundry and getting everybody ready. There were no complaints from the boys, big and small, but they sure weren't moving very fast either.

"John, Jacob!" she said again, "I am not going to be late, let's get going!"

J.L. was roused from his preoccupation with a cup of coffee at the kitchen table. He got up, headed for the door, "Maddie, I will have the buckboard ready in a shake" He said.

Meanwhile Maddie was nearly wrestling with Jacob to get his shirt on straight and a cow lick to lay down with a little mother's glue, her salvia.

Soon the family was on their way the quarter hour it would take to get to the church located in town. It was a beautiful day although a bit windy which flapped bonnet strings and a bow tie J.L. had put on. Maddie could not remember the last time she had seen him in one and wondered where got it. But it was warm and J.L. could feel the perspiration on his forehead under his hat and at the small of his back. He thought Maddie just seemed to glow and he remembered that she was still the prettiest thing on God's green earth. Jacob, scrunched between the two, talked up a storm with lots of questions about Goldendale and J.L.'s trip.

As they pulled in it seemed like everybody else had arrived at the same time. The service was at least fifteen minutes away from starting but it was time for friend and neighbor to catch up on a week's worth of news.

The Pastor was standing out front, greeting one and all. "Maddie, so nice to see you, and John, oh it is so good to see you, I have heard about your, uh, adventure, probably not the right word. But I am so glad you are safe. I sure would like an opportunity to visit this week."

"Certainly," Maddie said, "we would welcome that very much."

"Yes sir, I think that would be a very good thing," J.L. said, enthusiastically, realizing that now if anyone in the community could have a sense about this mission he was considering it would be the parson.

It was good to be in the church. Many people who were familiar with them greeted him like he was a long lost brother. He took comfort in the hymns that were sung, even ventured to sing although somewhat under his breath. Jacob was doing the best he could for a boy but there was a girl that seemed to have his eye, or visa-versa. Maddie elbowed him a couple of times, but smiled at J.L.

The pastor's sermon came from 2nd Corinthians the first chapter concentrating on the verses 3-11. *"Blessed be God, even the Father of our Lord Jesus Christ, the Father of mercies and the God of all comfort; Who comforteth us in all our tribulation that we may be able to comfort them which are in any trouble, by the comfort wherewith we ourselves are comforted of God."* This passage spoke to J.L. He wasn't exactly sure why it was, but it gave him a sense of the way God works through people, double duty sometimes. He certainly believed that his very own wife was a vessel of this kind of care. After all he was home when he really had done enough trouble to have rightly lost it all. He knew that Gideon showered this comfort and care on him and he was sure that there were many others that had been on the receiving end with Gideon.

Did God use special people for this as if they might be uniquely appointed he wondered, but did not know? He found it hard to imagine himself providing godly comfort although he certainly believed he had received it.

For Maddie it was a different passage that the pastor shared that she felt was what the Lord wanted her to hear especially with the dilemma at hand. *"Who delivered us from so great a death, and doth deliver in whom we trust that he will yet deliver us; Ye also helping together by bestowed upon us by the means of many persons that's may be given by man on our behalf."* verse 10&11

For Maddie there was a deep seated fear that she tried to keep buried. Although it would certainly come to the surface every time Clint Jeffers rose his ugly head to do more evil. As she had worried but kept quiet about was the fear that when J.L. left on the cattle drive to Mitchell that she would never see him again. And it wasn't just Jeffers but the job, the country and maybe even J.L.'s foolishness that he would fall off the wagon and the alcohol would get him.

Now, here she was faced with telling her husband to go off to some place called Hells Canyon to find one man to tell him that his father was dead and that some of that responsibility rested on J.L. And what about Jeffers again, was he waiting around some dark corner or would he follow her husband to Hells Canyon? Not only that, she began to wonder why this bad man was so intent. It didn't make sense that one person could be so crazy mad that he would go the distance and take the risk to try to kill her husband.

What she felt the Holy Spirit was attempting to tell her was that God was in charge and he would protect, and that she needed to put these fears away. And too that she needed to see a bigger picture. J.L. was becoming the man she hoped he would but more importantly he was becoming the man God wanted him to be. And it was not her place to get in front of that.

Some words from the bible she took great comfort in, most in fact. But some made her feel a little prickly, like she was being needled by God himself as if saying, "My child, you need to heed this and trust in me."

~~~

Once home the family gathered for Sunday dinner. Old Mr. Larson was invited. He regaled them all with tales of his days at sea and then as a mountain man. Jacob hung on every word, as did J.L. Maddie appreciated the stories and they were excited but she really wanted to talk with J.L. about the pastor's message. After dinner it was time for coffee and pie and all the boys, old boy, big boy and little boy began to look like they would be happy to settle in for a Sunday nap.

Mr. Larson rose up, a bit unsteady and thanked Maddie for her hospitality. "I need to be a goin', I am sure there is something I need to do before I call it a day." He seemed wobbly on his feet.

Maddie said, "Jacob, would you walk Mr. Larson home, maybe you can be a help to him for a bit."

"Sure, Ma," Said Jacob. He was hoping to see some more of what seemed to be an endless collection of artifacts and relics that Mr. Larson had acquired.

J.L. had now slumped in his chair, feet up, boots off and sleep was playing at his heavy eyelids.

Maddie came and set on the stool, next to him then changed her mind and scrunched in with him into the old chair, arms draped about him. "John, I know you would like a nap but can you give me a few minutes?"

J.L. perked up, thinking that Maddie was ready to talk about the proposition.

"Honey, what did you think of what the pastor had to say?"

"Well, it was good words but I still feel like I have a lot of learning to do but what hit me was that God uses others to provide ... a ... what was the word?"

"Comfort."

"Well, it helped me to see a little more about how God works, I think. Um, I first thought he has used you over the years with me, Jacob and others to give comfort. And he seemed to have comforted you in your times of trouble. I believe that to be true because you still believe in a good God and that people can be good."

"Do you see God using you that way?"

"Hard to imagine. It seems like I got to believe but I don't see how that has changed things. Gideon's dead, his son has a shot up knee, I only seem to be delivering pain and suffering."

"That's not so, John. I think we need to blame the one who is really causing the trouble."

"Jeffers."

"Yes him too. But the devil has put this violence on him to carry out."

"I think that you were exactly who God wanted to tell Gideon's family what happened. I don't know what exactly you said, but I believe it was a comfort to them rather than not."

J.L.'s reaction to this insight was to want to get away like it was all too much. He was a simple fellow, happy to be pounding out hot iron into something useful or searching for a stray calf out on the high plain. In fact, as much as he liked being close in Maddie's arms at that moment there was a feeling about how great it would be to be following a stream up into the hills, quiet, peaceful and with little to think about other than maybe yanking supper from a cool spring.

Maddie continued on while J.L. was trying to be distracted by a vision of wilderness in his mind. "And I don't think they would have entrusted you to such a task and given us all this money if they didn't see . . . um . . . God working in you, I guess." In the back of her mind, Maddie wanted to argue with her own words of encouragement. Not that she didn't believe in her husband, but that she was now convincing him he needed to go when that was in her own flesh the last thing she wanted him to do. She also had a thought pop into her head of contacting a certain Mr. & Mrs. Strother in Pendleton Oregon. In fact, as she also thought, she would go to the Western Union office tomorrow and wire them.

"John, what do you think?" She asked while squeezing him a little tighter to her."

J.L. did not answer, did not want to answer. He wanted his life back without this responsibility and yet he didn't want that old life back either. This God business had certainly come with blessings but at the same time the task ahead was more than he could imagine. He was not afraid to go into Hells Canyon, relished the idea really if he was a young buck with no responsibility. He was no longer thinking that a nap was going to happen, too much on his mind now.

He began to rise from the chair, trying not to dump Maddie on the floor while he did.

"Honey, where are you going?"

"Um, I think I need to take ole Gus for a ride. I guess I need a bit of time. Is that alright with you? I won't be gone long."

"Sure, I understand."

It was late in the day and so he did not plan to be gone for long. Gus saddled, J.L. turned his head west along the road that hugged rim of the Columbia gorge. The great river shimmered and shined in the sun of that late day. The wind had calmed down to but a whisper and just enough to keep him cool in the waning heat of the day. Below he could see a few fishermen plying the waters for 'springers'. The oaks and high pines provided intermittent shade as he rode. The air smelled sweet and wild flowers were still everywhere to be seen especially large yellow ones and purple ones growing together. He had no idea what they were other than pretty.

He had the road to himself as he navigated the highs and lows of it. He had come to believe that when God made Oregon he decided that the more hills and valleys the better because flat places were certainly hard to find.

He didn't know what he was exactly praying but his question to himself and to God was, "Is this what I am supposed to be doing? Is this somehow something to do with what your plans are with me, if you have that on your plan at all?"

The sky, rocks and river did not shout an answer. But then the words of the pastor this morning came back. Not the sermon but before that, "Can I pay you folks a visit this week?"

Counsel that is what Maddie and he needed. This was a man who knew about this sort of thing, J.L. imagined. Some how maybe he could make some sense of it all and put it into a perspective that would help them to make such a big decision.

J.L. thought, "Yes, this would be good." He also thought about the fact that this is not the kind of thing he would have thought before. You make your own decisions and you live with the results, right or wrong.

Chapter Three
A Journey Considered

"For I know the plans I have for you, declares the Lord, plans to prosper you and not to harm you, plans to give you hope and a future."
Jeremiah 29:11

The awaited knock came on the door on Thursday afternoon. J.L. and Maddie knew when Goliath barked a friendly greeting that Pastor Gilman had come for his promised visit. Maddie was busy trying to flatten down Jacob's cowlick and help him get his shirt tucked back into his trousers. J.L. was up from his chair to answer the door.

"Howdy pastor, good to see you" he said, nearly wrenching the good minister's hand and arm from its socket.

"Thank-you, J.L. Good to see you and Maddie. You too, young Jacob," he said as he extended his hand to the family, one at a time.

Maddie served coffee and cookies while they chit-chatted about life on their ranch, how the Pastor's wife was. She often suffered terrible headaches that kept her at home more than she would like. The Pastor had many questions for Jacob. Finally Maddie dismissed Jacob asking him to check on Mr. Larson.

"I get the sense that perhaps there is more on your mind?" the pastor prompted.

"Well, sir, that is true and we are glad for your visit today because, I guess we need a little advice. Uh, this is all kind of new to us," J.L. proceeded. He then went on to tell of his meeting and the incident with the Thomas family over in Goldendale and about the request for him to travel to the Snake River country came about.

"I guess what it comes down to", started Maddie, "simply put, should J.L. go? This is a hardship, true, he is being paid well for his task, but . . . I guess we are just trying to figure the Good Lord's will in all of this."

"I certainly can give you my opinion, and I may. You know, I have been praying for you folks for some time. It seems God puts you on my heart frequently and I have tried to be obedient to that and pray. I have not always been sure exactly what to pray for you about other than, J.L., your salvation and God's will in all of your lives. But today it became crystal clear to me. The Lord, I believe, provided me with a bible verse, just now, that I feel He would want me to share with you." The pastor said this while thumbing through his ancient and worn bible. "Let me just read this to you and you tell me what you think and then we can discussion it from there."

The pastor read from Second Thessalonians, chapter one, verses eleven and twelve, ***"Wherefore also we pray for you, that our God would count you worthy of this calling, and fulfill all the good pleasure of his*** *goodness, and the work of faith with power. That the name of our Lord Jesus Christ may be glorified in you, and in him, according to the grace of our God and the Lord Jesus Christ."*

The pastor let the words sink in a bit before saying anything additional.

Both Maddie and J.L. thought deeply, searching for what this meant and how it applied to them. Maddie was first to speak. "I think this is Paul talking, correct? And he is addressing this to a young man named Titus."

"Correct, Paul is reminding young Titus that he has been called to the Lord's work in Thessalonica. That he has been prayed for and that Paul expects that Titus will reveal through his calling to those people the Grace and Mercy of the Lord Jesus," the pastor affirmed.

"So, you are saying this is for me something similar, that I am called by the Lord to do this journey?" J.L asked.

"Perhaps, more importantly, is that you have been called to do his work. And more than just being a man of God as husband and father although, that is certainly enough of a calling of its own." The pastor's voice was calm, quiet but with a sense of reassurance.

Again, J.L. felt the sense of wanting to bolt, to head to the high hills or the blacksmith shop where it all seemed simpler. Maddie extended her hand and placed it on his, as a reassurance as if she was reading his mind. J.L. started to stand, which in turn made the pastor start to rise, but then he promptly sat back down and so did the pastor.

"Well, isn't that a fine howdy-you-do," said J.L. almost with a laugh and agitation in his voice. They both waited to see if J.L. was going to add anymore but he remained silent and staring through the pastor.

"Friends, I think I should be running along but let me pray with you before I go." At that he reached out his hand to grasp both of Maddie's fine small hand and J.L.'s ham-hock of a hand. "Lord, I thank Thee for this couple and all that you have been doing in their lives. I thank Thee for your miraculous ways and for what you have ordered for their lives in you. I thank you for the mission you are providing for them both. Lord give the Matthews peace about your plans for them, so as they step into this new way that they will rest in you for your way. Amen."

"I have one other verse to share with you. It is one I have oft meditated on for my own life especially in challenging time. This is found in Jeremiah chapter twenty nine, verse eleven, *"For I know the plans I have for you I have for you, declares the Lord, plans to prosper you and not to harm you, plans to give you hope and a future."*

~~~

The next morning, Maddie rose early, telling J.L. and Jacob she had shopping to do in town. But she did not take the buckboard, instead saddled her horse, grabbed a saddle bag of J.L's and flew to town enjoying the sun on her back and the breeze in her hair. Her first stop was the Western Union office. In a short message from Maddie
Matthews to Mr. Robert Strother of Pendleton Oregon she simply said, "If you want that stud you desire it's yours for one hundred dollars, delivered STOP".

She didn't think she had prayed over a Western Union wire before but she did now, and rather sheepishly. "Lord, I shan't prevent you from sending my husband to the Snake River. I just ask that you make part of the way there for me too. Uumm, Amen."

Next she stopped by the mercantile for a few things and then was back on her horse and heading back for home. This time she took her time a bit, just to enjoy the morning, the breeze rustling at her unhindered auburn hair.

J.L. was a little slow to get up. He had tossed and turned much of the night it seemed. He was excited, anxious and full of wonder for what he was about to set off to do. And it wasn't just this long trip to find a needle in a haystack of a man to tell him his father was dead it was the stops along the way to try to communicate to others the last days of Gideon. And somehow, he suspected, to share what God did and was doing in his own life.

"Why if that just don't beat all", he said, aloud but to only the morning sun. This was truly words of disbelief and doubt that he was on some sort of path to serve God in some way. In fact, he railed against the idea of such a ludicrous thing.

His best thought for the time being was to put it out of his mind and get done what needed to be done around the place and plan for the trip. He was of a mind to get on with it by Monday next, five days away.

As he began morning chores of feeding stock horses, oxen, cattle and there always seemed to be a growing menagerie of animals especially in the horse department. Maddie was a true horse trader and it seemed he could go out some morning and spot one corralled that he had not noticed before and one or two missing from the last time. He knew Maddie had a real hankering to be a horse breeder and she was well along in being a fine trainer. On occasion folks would drop a mustang by with the hopes that Maddie, in her quiet words and ways, to get the ornery one to settle down and be of some use.

After the feeding of the stock, J.L. rousted Jacob to come out and take care of the poultry. He didn't know what Maddie was planning for breakfast but a few eggs would do well. Next J.L. set about to milking Ginny the milk cow. They had acquired her some years back. She was gentle and had birthed a lot of calves over the years. As J.L. began the process, sitting on a milk stool that looked like it could collapse under his girth; in a second the cats arrived, half a dozen of them, some he knew, others guests of the ones Maddie claimed as hers.

Now and then J.L. would turn a teat towards the gathered assembly and shoot warm milk their way. There was always a lot of licking of whiskers, ears and paws after. Goliath soon joined the party and quickly learned from the cats how to make the best of it.

While he was about this business Maddie had arrived home and was soon clanging around in the kitchen and the aroma of ham, eggs, biscuits and coffee found it's way into the barn.

Soon the family was gathered for breakfast. Maddie was insistent on a lengthy time of grace this morning. In part she prayed for what she would normally pray for on this summer morning. As she continued she seemed to begin to really implore upon the Lord. "Father, you seem to have a course set before us that we can not see very much of, just a few steps ahead. And maybe it's not our affair to know more of that. But I would ask you most humbly to please let us have an assurance that what John is about to undertake and the words from the pastor yesterday will helps us to . . . a . . . rest in you. We move blindsided in this a bit. Well, Sir, we just need to trust and obey but for that bit of trust we extend we would like to feel that blessed assurance that this is what you have for us."

It seemed no sooner than she had finished and they had begun to eat, J.L. gobbling one whole egg at a time, a lad of Jacob's age showed up at the door. He had a slip of paper in his hand. "Mrs. Matthews, I am from the Western Union office and Bud said I should get this to you pronto."

"Why, thank you Son," said Maddie, looking for a coin or two to tip the boy who was soon out on his way back.

Maddie sat down, stared at the paper for a bit while J.L. and Jacob stared at her. She then opened it with a snap. Took a quick look, there was one word and it was "Deal". She exclaimed "Glory be!" Gobbling a couple of bites and rising again she said, "Boy's I will be back in a jiffy", as she bounded out of the house.

"Pa?" Jacob started.

"I don't know, but I am sure she will tell us soon enough. We got a lot to get done today so eat up." And they did, J.L. finished what was on Maddie's plate not wanting it to go to waste he rationalized.

There was a bit of fence that needed repair, there was always the ditch for the irrigating to keep clear and there was some blacksmith work to be done to keep the old buckboard in one piece or at least road ready.

~~~

At the end of that long and warm day the family gathered for a late supper, but this time outside, under the shade of a large oak. A breeze was kicking up off the gorge. It had been too hot to spend much time around the kitchen stove when Maddie returned early in the afternoon. So the meal was sliced bread, cheese, roast beef, fresh pickles from the Mercantile and a pile of greens, young carrots, etc. from the garden. Under a towel something hid that looked like it must be dessert.

Once they had commenced their supper, J.L. spoke up, "You going to tell us, Maddie?"

"You know that appaloosa I got out there?"

"The stud, yeah, real spirited."

"A while back I met a couple at the church from Pendleton, after the service we were talking about horses and I told him about the 'Appie'. He wanted to see him, liked what he saw and I think would have bought him on the spot if it for not being able to transport him back to Pendleton from where they were from. They were visiting family here. Well, I wired them this morning and told him if he still wanted that horse for a hundred dollars that I would deliver him.

That is what that message was about," said Maddie while producing the note from her apron pocket. She handed it to J.L. who read the one word.

"You are . . ."

"Let me finish. I then went to Mrs. Valdez, who by the way provided this dessert, bless her heart. And then I stopped off at the Decker's, you know they got all those teen boys. Well," Maddie took a deep breath here. "Mrs. Valdez is going to come and stay for a while and Josh, is going to come over and help Jacob every day because Mr., I am going as far as Pendleton with you."

"Uh?", J.L. started to protest but then on second thought and knowing it would do no good and on third thought, this is really good. "So you ride to Pendleton with me and then how are you getting back because . . ."

"I will take the stage, it is just one over night and then I will be home in a week's time."

"Well, you know what, I got my own trip to make to the Western Union . . . a, because I told the Thomas' I would get back to them after I talked with you, and it looks like you've decided it."

Maddie gave J.L. a questionable look as if to say, 'I thought this was already decided.' But then decided the Lord's hand had been in this altogether and now it was set. But what did Jacob think. "Honey", she said, turning her eyes on her son who sat silent but with a look of wonder on his face. "What do you think about this?"

"I am alright with this . . . I think." The big boy in him was quite excited, yet the little boy was feeling a bit apprehensive. "You'd just be gone a week, right, Ma?"

"Yes, son, that is all it should take."

Then Jacob looked at his father about to ask a similar question.

"I am sorry, Son. But I will be gone longer, maybe a month."

"But you havta do it don't ya, Paw."

"Yep, I got to get to town and why don't you come with. I got an idea bouncing on my noggin that I need your help with."

"Sure" and soon the two men in Maddie's life were on ole Gus headed for town and some adventure she would probably learn about later.

J.L. stopped first at the Western Union to wire the Thomas' that he would be heading out on Monday. Next he stopped at the Marshall's office to let them know he and Maddie would be out of town and what for and to ask that they be aware of who was staying at the place in light of all that had gone on. Next they proceeded to the hardware store but instead of buy goods to do more repair and projects both of them stopped to look in the display window at the newest fishing equipment. They ogled a rod and reel that seemed to hold much promise.

"Is that the one you want Son?" J.L. asked.

"Yes", said Jacob with his eyes still glued on the angling wonder.

"Well, lets' go get it and see if we can't catch your Ma enough supper to feed an army."

Back home, J.L. found his old rod while Jacob looked for night crawlers down around the creek. Soon they were back on Gus, a big lunch tucked inside the saddle bag from Maddie and they were headed for river?

It was a short trip, J.L. had in mind a spot where the river eddied into a little inlet. It would be safe and the fish might be resting in there. He helped Jacob get rigged up, put a bobber on the line, flung it out and told Jacob to watch that bobber. "You will know when the fish comes a knockin' that bobber will start to popping up and down." He then baited his hook and cast the line out to the middle of the eddy, where the line would drift with it, hoping that it would entice a lunker.

While there the two noticed an old wagon just up from them, half hidden among the willows. Then an old lady appeared, she was comely but portly. She wore a man's broad-brim and denims and she was carrying a large trout or steelhead. She hollered out, "Leland, you got to help me with this thing?" An old man, large and tall appeared from out of some bushes, peering through a pair of spectacles. "What you say?" he said, while cupping a hand to his ear.

"I got another one, you going to help with this and what are you doing in the bushes anyway?"

"I'm a coming Kate!" said the old man, while trotting to her, but his foot hit a root in the ground and down he went, head over heals.

J.L. was concerned that the old fellow had hurt himself and took off to see if he could help but before he got there the man named Leland was up on his feet and continuing on to help his wife.

J.L. got to them in a second. "You alright there, sir?"

"Why sure, fine as frog's hair." Leland assured as he and Kate struggled to get the hook out of the squirming fish.

"They're hittin' real good in there Pa, you need to come check your line."

"Sure, sure, just a minute, I got to dig up something I found yonder." And Leland was back into the brush.

"Crazy ole coot", said Kate, more to herself. "Howdy, big fella, my name is Kate and that fella with his backside stickin' out of the brush is my husband Leland."

"Nice to meet ya," said J.L., extending a paw to shake her small hand.

"I am J.L. and that boy over there, watching the bobber like a hawk, is my son Jacob." Then he asked, "Are you folks from around here?" noticing the old covered wagon that looked like it had traveled the Oregon Trail and back again.

"Oh, here, there, everywhere I suppose but yes we do have a little spread a mile down river. We been kinda gypsies for Jesus for so long, home seems to be where we lay our heads at night." All the time during this she cleaned the fish like she could have done it blinded fold. She then mounted it on a heavy stick, secured at an angle over a fire. There were a few other fish hung there. They were being cooked over some hot coals.

"You and your boy hungry? It won't be long, we've plenty to share."

"Ma'am, the Missus packed us some dinner, so no, but thanks anyway."

"Fish don't taste better than this way and ole Leland will probably find something over yonder in those bushes to add to it."

And as if on cue Leland popped back out of the bushes with his arms full of all kinds of green things. "Look Ma, wild onions, chicory, cattails and some other groceries!"

He was soon back and with his knife cutting and trimming the wild vegetables he found. He placed them in a cast iron skillet with butter and soon the smell of those greens wafted through the air.

Jacob was beginning to get bored watching that bobber than sat motionless. He wandered over to meet the couple. "Boy, that sure smells good Ma'am."

"Good, cause we want to share." J.L. nodded that it would be alright for them to join the old couple.

Soon Kate and Leland, whose last name was Harrison, had set out an old cloth on the ground, found enough tin plates and cutlery to made do for the four of them. She piled on fish while Leland piled on a mess of succulent greens.

"You mind if I say a little blessing?" said Leland.

"Not at all," Answered J.L.

Leland and Kate took off there hats, bowed their heads, closed there eyes, as did J.L. and Jacob. Then Leland said, "Thank you Jesus, Amen." and that was it for grace.

As they ate J.L. asked about the Harrison's. They had served in ministry in one form or another for years. Much of it had to do with street ministries to the forlorn on skid row in Portland and other cities or with orphans and abandoned children. Now they had retired.

J.L. asked how they spent their time now, "Well, I've been painting" said Kate, producing a number of paintings done on boards. And Leland, well, he spends a lot of time looking in the bushes. In fact he wrote a little book about it."

Kate's artwork was primitive but with much expression. J.L. noted a painting she did of the rocks and hills not too far from where his ranch was. Meanwhile Jacob looked at Leland's little book which was full of drawings, sketches and descriptions of plant and herbs and what to do with them. The title of the book was "God's Bounty".

"So this is what you do for a living now?" J.L. asked.

"Well, the old man is veteran of the high seas and the Indian wars in his earlier days so he draws a little pension but we don't so much worry about that. We work at living these days and let the Good Lord worry about the making part."

"Do you sell your paintings, Kate?" J.L. was kind of hankering after that one painting, "and can we get one of your books Leland, I think my Maddie would like to read that."

"Why sure we do." Leland was up and searching through the wagon for a copy of the book.

"What would be fair payment?"

Kate looked at J.L. hard, "Son, I don't quite know how to say this but in my spirit I feel as if God has something planned for you that you think is too big to do . . . it is just what I feel. What I would like from you is this, is that you listen close to what the Lord says, in His word, through the Holy Ghost who is contending with you, from those around you who are listening to the Lord and that you do what God wants you to do. And don't worry about your ability to do it. Would you promise me that, don't say, "No I can't to God."

Her statement stopped J.L. in his tracks. He was quiet for a bit, as was his fashion. "Ma'am, I don't know how you knew it, but that has been on my mind all day but I have not shared it with a single soul. I want to do as you say. I will give it my best and in some way that I can not understand I think the Lord gave you and Leland to us today."

Shortly after the makeshift meal, the old couple was on their way. "We've got kids, grandkids and great grandkids spread all across this state and we are on our way to visit each and all of them this summer."

"And Boys, if you expect to catch any fish, then there are a few things that you need to do," said Kate and she shared a few of her nuances in catching fish.

After they left and with all that Kate said, both boys caught enough fish and some. J.L. also heard in his spirit an old verse he thought he had long forgotten. "I will make you fishers of men."

Chapter Four
An Unexpected Journey

"For I am already being poured out like a drink offering, and the time has come for my departure."
2nd Timothy 4:5

The next few days went so quickly with chores, duties and last minute things to do to get ready for the trip that Monday snuck up on them fast. Mrs. Valdez had shown up early, brought in by one of her sons in an old buckboard filled with some new cut hay and her small bag pitched on top. Some of the Decker boys, along with Mr. Decker would be over later in the day.

Maddie had made enough French toast to last today and tomorrow for Jacob plus enough for them tomorrow morning. She had made biscuits, snicker doodles and pretty much anything else she could think of for Jacob and Mrs. Valdez and the hungry Decker boys who would show up to help. She tried to have enough provisions of dried fruit, jerky and coffee to get them through for the days they would be out but not so much that travel would be hard. Her hope was that J.L. would bag supper a few times to make it easier.

Finally it was time to leave. Jacob was doing his best to not show he was afraid or worried but to J.L. he looked like such a little boy. He knew Maddie probably felt the same way. When she hugged and kissed Jacob it was hard for her to let go of him.

"Ma, I'll be fine," said Jacob, puffing out his chest.

Mrs. Valdez put her arms around Maddie and Jacob's and saying "Senor, I pray, I pray now for your safe journey."

The hope was to get twenty miles or so that first day, it would probably become less after that as the horses endured the strain. They would walk and rest the horses as often as seemed possible. As they rode along the Gorge country, it became more barren and less green. This was a place of bare hills, jagged rocks and where green living things existed closer to the river and the creeks that fed it. They forded the Deschutes River some half mile up stream from the mouth of the river where it ran shallow and wide. They let the horses drink and this was a good place to stop and stretch a spell.

J.L. decided to try his luck with a long willow he cut along the bank and some string and a hook he brought along just in case. He flayed the water quite a bit until he could settle into a rhythm. Up and down the stream he walked, often wading in up to the tops of his boots but the water seemed empty. He then spied a spot where the water eddied around an ancient log. Here he tried and lo and behold if he didn't get a strike and a fat trout took to the air. There was another one in quick order after that and while he would have liked to keep fishing he thought this would be enough. He cleaned them by the river bank and wrapped them in soaking wet burlap to keep them cool until they would stop that night.

As they neared a little community they could see off some distance, they found a little canyon where some water ran and there were trees. They picked out a spot, gathered some firewood. Maddie took to boiling a few potatoes she brought along, gathered some greens by the creek she said were edible and J.L. took the trout, mounted on sticks at angle and cooked them over the embers of the fire. Maddie did not remember when fish tasted so good, J.L. agreed but wished for another potato and the greens, well they were okay too.

They found a spot near a large Ponderosa Pine that had dropped ample needles. This they bunched up in to a soft mound and placed their bedrolls on top. Gus and the other horse were hobbled for the night. Goliath fed on jerky and biscuits while deciding the most comfortable place was between Maddie and J.L. This ruined any idea of a romantic interlude under the stars. They, however, were all quite tired and soon sound sleep.

This schedule went on for a few more days. Sometimes J.L. would catch some fish, sometimes he would be blessed with a sage hen or a couple of cottontails.

At Boardman they left the river and headed cross country with the hope of making it to Pendleton in two more days. There was a certain sadness or loss of comfort in striking off and away from the Columbia that neither expressed but felt. As it was getting on to late afternoon they came across a substantial stream. J.L. wasn't sure but believed this to be the Umatilla River. Here a population of people lived and farms and ranches were to be found along the river's banks.

They pulled up to area and noticed a young boy and an older fellow down by the steam, they were fishing and it appeared they were doing quite well. The young boy was quick to want to show all the fish they had caught and the older gentlemen, the boy's grandfather, had a quick smile and a 'how do you do'.

Before long, the grandfather invited them to his place where he lived with his wife and the boy. Turns out the boys parents had died in an accident and now the grandparents were raising him.

The wife found more plates and soon Maddie and J.L. were enjoying quite a dinner and warm conversation. The house was small but they took up the invitation to stay in the barn. A big mound of hay looked like a very comfortable spot after nights on pine needles or less.

J.L. and Maddie were up early, trying to get going before the Palmer family thought they ought to be feeding breakfast to their visitors as well. But that didn't work. Mr. Palmer was right there as they began to saddle up and told them breakfast was just minutes away. Although the day promised to be a warm one, it was cool this morning even making Maddie give out a shudder. J.L. noticed and reached in the saddlebag and pulled out Gideon's old black frock and draped it around her shoulders. She snuggled into it gratefully. As they came into the house Mrs. Palmer was there to greet them. Her face was red and she had an apron on. An unruly lock of hair was playing across her worn face and there seemed to smudge off flour on her chin. Maddie instinctively reached out to wipe it off. The kindly woman said with a little embarrassment. "Oh, I must look a sight. I am sure you are hungry, and the coffee is ready."

They were soon gathered around the table. The old man extended his weathered hands as to grasp the nearest hand next to him as well did Mrs. Palmer. He prayed a short but beautiful prayer, grateful in thanksgiving for the life they had. As they ate, J.L. noticed that the two kept staring at Maddie. He didn't mind, he liked to look upon her too, especially in the morning. The couple would soon notice that they were staring and then turn away as if in embarrassment. J.L. thought for a moment, and remembered his own incident like this . . . because of the coat that was draped around Maddie's shoulders.

He said, "I am a figuring that maybe that coat that Maddie has on is familiar to you."

"Oh," said the Mrs. Palmer, "Um yes, and pardon me so much for staring."

"Did you folks know the circuit rider, Rev. Thomas?"

"Why, yes, we did, um, is that his coat? He has visited us on occasion over the years, especially with the passing of this little boy's Ma and Pa."

Once again J.L. imparted the story of Gideon's last days. He began to realize that this was something he might do for some while to come. It gave him second thoughts in that he must always tell the whole of the story when appropriate to make sure that he gave the man the respect he deserved. After all, J.L. realized, he was on a mission. Perhaps it wasn't to carry on in the footsteps of Gideon Thomas, that notion seemed remote at best. But it was his task to tell the story of this fine man's last days and what they meant to him and his family. He cared little about sharing his own testimony, per se, nothing much to be proud of there. More importantly how this man lived his life right up to the end.

After J.L. shared his story, Maddie adding a bit, the room was quiet. The boy had gone out to play. Goliath was sleeping near by.

"You know, last night I thought I knew that dog. We had seem him once before but I couldn't quite place it. If you wouldn't mind, tell us again where you are headed."

"Well, first to Pendleton and then I am heading on alone to the Snake River, that great canyon that lies beyond Farewell Bend." And before they could ask, "I am going on to find Gideon's oldest son, to tell him of his loss. I was also asked by the family to tell those folks I might find about Gideon so I guess, uh, maybe the Good Lord arranged this?" J.L. suddenly felt sheepishly for saying such a thing but the folks were quick to respond.

"A divine appointment I think" said Mrs. Palmer then added, "I'm a guessing, young man, you have not come to peace about this matter."

"Well", J.L. started. Maddie put her hand on his beneath the table.

"This morning, I was thinking of a bible verse when I woke up. I thought it might be for me. We sure are not getting any younger and we have this boy to take care. Sometimes it seems too much although we wouldn't change it for a minute. But, maybe, this is for you two. Give me a moment to find it, will you?" Mr. Palmer said, as he went to retrieve a worn family bible. He thumbed through for a bit until he came to the second letter to Timothy from the Apostle Paul.

"Here it is, "'For I am now ready to be offered and the time of my departure is at hand.'". I thought about that for us, we are old, our days are numbered, it is like we can see the sands of time run out faster everyday. Yet Paul saw his life as a sacrifice and I don't think much more. I don't think this is how we saw our golden years playing out raising this youngun', but I wouldn't trade it for a minute. I don't think Paul was any different, in fact much more so that most of us I reckon. Let me read you the rest." "'I have fought the good fight, I have finished the race, I have kept the faith.'" As best as I can figure it, Gideon's number was up, he had been poured out, like an offering, back there in those Painted Hills. He had completed his journey and task. The events that took place there, the bad man, your circumstances, were just a part of his great mission. And now you are called to tell this story, maybe more. I don't want to sound preachy, we will leave that for the men in the pulpits but I think for me today, to visit these verses and in light of what you have told us is somehow and encouragement. You know, by golly, I will not lose site of my chore of fighting the good fight, finishing the race and keeping the faith with the hope that it will mean something to that little boy out there when we are long gone off to heaven."

J.L. and Maddie gave a second wave to their smiling hosts as they departed. It was quickly turning into a hot one and that was the way with this country. You could be down right chilled in the morning but with in a few hours the perspiration was rolling down your forehead, neck and back. The would take it a little easy today, maybe ten to fifteen miles with a long break in the afternoon and then traveling into the late afternoon right up to twilight.

They would follow the Umatilla River all the way to Pendleton, probably forty miles away. This way water would be available all day in places here and there. Hopefully they could camp along its banks and maybe a little fishing for supper right at the end of the day.

Other than the river and the vegetation that choked around it this was a barren land they crossed, rolling hills, jagged cliffs and not much for water or people just a few

ranches and farms dotting the landscape here and there. At places the Umatilla dropped into canyons and it was a ridge ride.

After they settled into the ride Maddie asked J.L. what he thought of these folks they spent the night with and the old gentlemen's little sermon.

"They were the nicest folks, offered real Christian hospitality as my Mama would say."

"They certainly did that, bless their hearts," Maddie added.

"And it was good that we met those folks so we could tell them about Gideon, that divine appointment stuff is a bit of a stretch for me but who knows. As far as his little talk, that I liked. I look at this big ole bible some times, all these pages, words that are a bit over my head so when I hear something that is simple it helps. I am a simple man and these are three things I can consider. There is a fight and it is between good and evil and we can be on either side. Life feels a bit like a foot race sometimes and you wonder about quitting the race and just being happy on the sidelines. And the faith part, well, I guess God takes care of that. I don't know much about faith but sometimes I think I see some glimpses of it in action."

"Yes, the dirt simple gospel is good, helps you to focus. John, I don't think you are that simple. I think maybe there is much that goes on in your noggin and probably more in the days to come."

"Maddie, my sweet, you give me more credit than I deserve."

By the end of that long day they got there fifteen miles in. The best part was a dip in the cool water in a place under the willows and a nap under those very same trees. Now it was way past dinner time and J.L. was thinking this stream had to old some trout or catfish or something. And it did and he caught one good sized cat and a couple of pan sized trout that smelled so good cooking in the lard that he could hardly wait. Maddie, mean time, hip deep in the water pulled up what she called Wapato or Duck Potatoes. Wapato was the Indian name she had heard, Duck Potatoes was about what you had to be to get to them. She gathered quite a few plus a half dozen new green cattails. These she boiled in the water and thanked the Lord, at dinner, for supplying all their needs that night from the very spot they chose to rest. J.L. relished the catfish the most, its white meat was succulent and rich but those river vittles were pretty good he had to admit. The cattails they ate like one would corn on the cob and the duck potatoes, well, like potatoes.

They were up the next morning nearly before the sun which was rising early. They were on the trail with just a couple of biscuits and coffee. J.L. figured another full day and they would be in Pendleton or at least close enough to see its lights.

They settled in for that night near the river but up on a ridge, they could see a few lights blinking in the night not more than a quarter mile away. This they believed was Pendleton. It wasn't really a full town yet but J.L. guessed more than a wide spot in the road when they crossed through the first time nearly eight years ago. This night they settled for a meager dinner of jerky and biscuits, Goliath looked like he was feeling deprived although he ate the lion's share. J.L. promised a real breakfast to Maddie the next morning at a café he hoped they might find.

The next morning Maddie took a little longer to get ready for town and also with meeting the Strothers. She wasn't exactly dressed for Sunday go-to-meeting but if ever someone graced a pair of trousers and a frilly blouse it was her. She passed on the old broad brim she had borrowed from J.L. rather had her hair braided in the back.

Pendleton wasn't much, not as big as The Dalles but the main street with its shops were a pleasant site. They found a café near the middle of town. Gus was given a feed bag with the last of the oats and Goliath was told to stay by the door. He looked as if he couldn't believe it when the inside seemed to smell so good. In a bit J.L. brought out to the dog a mess of scrambled eggs and a warmed up steak.

Back inside the coffee was hot and good and the sumptuous breakfast of steak, eggs and flap jacks hit the spot. The waitress, named Molly, was friendly and seemed to know every one who entered. Maddie to the chance to inquire about the whereabouts of the folks she planned to sell her horse to. Molly knew and gave directions. They actually lived back down in the valley they had come from, on the banks of the Umatilla just a short stretch from town.

They had a large ranch, which spread on both sides of the little river. There were cattle, horses, and some sheep and of course a selection of draft animals to get the day's work done.

Maddie and J.L., Goliath trotting along, entered through the wide gate a sign over head announced the name of the ranch. There was commotion in a field to the left as a few cowboys were busy rounding a small herd for what looked like to be a morning of branding, marking and cutting. A tall, older gentleman sat a horse and was waving and whistling at the border collies that were helping with the work to keep the herd together and heading for the stockade and chute. Through a series of commands he directed each dog to perform his task.

It wasn't so common to see working dogs like this, but more and more ranchers were trying them. Some of this was to the chagrin of some of the cowpokes who figured they could lose their jobs to some dogs that only asked for a meal and a place to sleep and an occasional pat on the head. Not all thought that way, happy for the help and to save on some sweat and wear and tear on boots and feet.

A short red haired lady was also out helping as well, she seemed as busy as a bee. Maddie recognized the tall man and the small lady as the Strothers. She had met them in The Dalles at church a year ago she thought, then coincidently, near her and J.L.'s place.

She had taken the horse to be purchased on a ride on the road to get him more used to others, wagons and riders. On that particular day he was not acclimating so well and was bucking and shying away as anything would near him. One couple that did, in their wagon, was these very same folks that she had met at church that morning.

She noticed them but had her hands full and could only give them a weak smile as they approached. Rather than passing by, Mr. Strother stopped the wagon and handed the reins to Mrs. Strother. He dismounted and slowing walked up to Maddie, hand extended, and the horse noticed and stop it's shenanigans to stare at the man. He held the horses gaze while approaching and then hardly without noticing took hold of the bridle. He whispered in a low voice and the horse grew quiet and Maddie could feel the tension in the powerful horse slip away.

"Thank you very much, um I am sorry, your name as escaped me."

"Robert Strother, ma'am, and pleased to meet you again, actually you are exactly who we were looking for."

"Oh?" said Maddie.

"We got to talking to some of the folks from the church about some horses for sale, and your name came up."

The horse and the rancher seemed to hit it off in those moments. "If you a mind to, I would like to purchase that horse from you when you are through with your training and he has a little more experience under this belt."

He then explained that they were from Pendleton, Maddie indicated that she would see what she could do but it didn't seem likely taking the horse all the way to Pendleton and all. But as providence or fortune would have it, here they now were.

Maddie and J.L. watched the commotion for a while. J.L. would have loved to have helped. Mrs. offered the two coffee and that could not be turned down. Soon Mr. Strother took his leave and joined them. He invited them into his study. Mrs. Strother fetched more coffee and some fresh baked cookies. J.L. was thinking, as much as he loved the trail and the open country, genteel surroundings sure were nice.

The deal was struck and money exchanged. Mr. Strother invited the Matthews to stay the night and they were happy to accept. A bath for both, supper and a little rest in the shade of an ancient willow was sweet. Later that evening as things began to cool the four of them mounted up and took off for to see the place and the surrounding area. They rode along the river and then up on a bluff to take in the valley. It seemed a fertile place for this desert land.

The next morning J.L. and Maddie were up early, they had a quick breakfast with the ranch couple but were eager to leave for town and the stage which left in a couple of hours. Maddie was mostly quiet during the ride. J.L. tried bits of conversation but didn't get too far in penetrating her silence.

"I know what you are thinking Maddie – well, I think. I don't really want to go, to leave you and Jacob behind. It is a little much to think about finding Joseph. I am not so sure offering to do with was the best. But, I've got to now . . ."

"John, it's alright, I was just thinking about days and nights, and how many will it be? Do I even want to guess and count? Of course you have to do this that is settled with me. But it is like I lost you, I got you back and now I am losing you again and this time, I don't know how long. Would you do something for me each night that you can, I will do the same as best I can. At nine o'clock each night, just before we turn in, would you go out and look at the stars. Maybe find the big dipper or the moon if it is out and just look at them, think what it was like a couple of nights back as we lay together and watched the heavens. I will do the same and some silly way, maybe we won't feel so far apart. I am not going to count the days, but just don't make it too many."

They soon found the stage line and, as far as J.L. was concerned, before he wanted to. Maddie boarded with others. There were a couple of other men, a small older fellow and a young fellow dressed as if he was going away too. There was a young woman and a little girl. Somehow J.L. knew that Maddie would take to them.

He made a stop at the mercantile, loaded up on bacon, jerky, some flour and sugar, coffee and other necessities. He would have liked to brought more but would wait till he got to Baker City. And from there he would make his entrance into the Snake River Canyon.

Today was a steep climb up into the Blue Mountains. It would take him much of the day to make the summit and perhaps a bit beyond. He remembered this place as a wild and solitary place. It did not know if there were now ranches in its highlands. Winters would be tough here. On the steep sections, and there was certainly enough of those, he walked giving Gus a breather. Goliath did his best to keep up but now a little cool grass under a tree was just too inviting.

They all kept at it though, J.L. wanting to make the top and if possible to get on the down hill side so that he could be in LaGrande the next day. From there, he estimated, it would be two days to Baker City where he would spend a day and then on into a great unknown.

    J.L., atop Gus, and Goliath moved on. The road he followed was that of the Oregon Trail, rutted form hundreds of wagon over forty years. It made it tough for walking and Gus would trip in the ruts. There were also muddy sections that made movement difficult with much slipping and sliding. J.L. decided he would have to walk much of it. And it wasn't walking it was plodding. Somewhere along the way he stepped wrong, lost his footing and took a hard fall that left him winded. He noticed that the pain in his back, the place where the old piece of lead from the rifle, was beginning to aggravate his muscles and his nerves and with each step it became worse.

    But he determined to make the summit at least and find a place up there to hole up for the night. By the time the three, man and beasts, made the top and found sufficient cover amongst huge Ponderosa pines the sun was setting. It wasn't cold but there was a bit of wind that was chilling on his sweat covered body. J.L. got a fire going, just a small one to keep them company through the night. Where he was, he saw no signs of life, human that is. Off to the East he could see the tracks where the wagons had maneuvered the hills. It suspected he would not have to look far to find some remnants of some of the wagons that didn't make it.

    In this place, because of a low spot in the ground there was water. And so there were also plenty of tracks, some from shod horses, others, Indian ponies but there were the wild animal prints too. Deer, surely but prints and scat from bear. Large cat tracks and the tracks of large dogs which had to believe were wolves. It made him edgy and he built the small fire a little higher although a little heat was all that was needed.

    Gus could find plenty of grass and Goliath and he made due with jerky and hardtack. He wasn't up for trying to spot some small game. The pain in his back that now shot up into his neck and all the way through his legs and feet was becoming excruciating. He hated to think what he might do if a bottle of whiskey would miraculously appear.

    On this first night out away from Maddie and a week gone from Jacob the thought of this trek he was in a bad way. He wished to be anywhere but here. He tried to find a comfortable spot in his bedroll after he and Goliath ate. Gus was hobbled and so would not travel far and J.L. was sure the horse was bushed as well. He wasn't old but he certainly wasn't young anymore either.

He hoped for sleep but this place was a reminder to him of the last leg of the journey, in fact he knew he had passed this very place before. He began to think that perhaps the small body of his lost child, died of the fever, was buried not too far off but he didn't know. Maddie had been at death's door and Jacob was so young on this trip. And when the baby died, the kindly folks took care of the body, gave a proper burial while J.L. looked on from a distance trying to console a very ill and heartbroken wife.

Now he could look at life and think that the move to out west was good. Finally life was something to be appreciated. But what if they hadn't moved rather had stayed in Virginia. Would life have been different, maybe even better? The war changed so much,

his parents killed. He and Maddie left family behind that they had not seen since. Some had migrated to the west also but no place close to see them.

J.L. began to drift off to sleep, Goliath close beside. But it wasn't good and restful sleep it was like what had happened so many times before. The war invaded his mind and dreams, reality and the oddity of dream life mixing with one another to torture him

And there came noises in the night too, it took him a while to come to from the depths of his nightmares to realize that Goliath was on his feet and growling deeply. It was a growl of warning and almost sounded if there was fear in his voice too. As J.L. woke more he could hear plainly what was disturbing. It was the sounds of dogs, not the cry of the coyote but that of wolves. It was hard to tell how close or far, the little hollow he was in carried the sound well.

He reached for his rifle which he had thought was right there with him but it was not to be found. He added more wood to the fire to try to brighten the dark night. He then remembered that when he had unsaddled Gus that he laid the rifle crooked up against a tree some twenty paces away. But in the dark he could not tell which tree. A dozen Ponderosa giants surrounded the sink that he had made camp in. Were the wolves that close, he did not know but he knew he needed that carbine.

He piled more wood on the fire, too much really, the heat forcing him and Goliath away from the protection of the fire. But in that moment as he looked into the darkness he saw of glint of orange fire on metal. He figured it was no more than ten paces to where he needed to be. Goliath however continued his growling. Gus, though, was not to be heard and he was not sure if the wolves had gotten to him or if he managed to get farther away, hidden in the thickets, even with the hobbles.

"I've got to get to that gun," he said to himself. And there was something about saying those words that propelled him up, running, not well, too much pain and then to sliding down to where the gun was. He had it in his hands but at that very moment something grabbed his wrist, sharp teeth dug in and he could feel them puncture through his skin just above his wrist. He started to try to rip his hand from the wolf's mouth but thought twice thinking that would only do more damage. The wolf snarled and yanked on his arm. This arm was extended up and away with the wolf holding on. "What to do" he thought, in a flash. He reached his other had out and was able to grab the rifle buy the barrel. Once he had it he swung it hard and hit the wolf somewhere in the body. It did not let go of his arm. He did again, and then again and once more before the wolf let go.

With that he was able to reach the rifle now with both hands and let out a shot in what he hoped was the direction of the wolf. The gun fired, the recoil echoed in the dark and he heard a yip from the wolf This seemed to push Goliath into action and he took a giant leap towards the dark but J.L. caught him in mid air, and pulled him to the ground, holding on to him for dear life. He held on for some time until Goliath settled down.

He drug himself back to the fire, took his bandana and not looking at his forearm wrapped it around his bloodied arm. He thought he should see about Gus but then he could hear the nickering of the horse nearby and so he was convinced that he was alright.

His arm hurt along with everything else but exhausted and in some shock, J.L. again fell fitfully asleep.

Some while later a voice spoke, "Mr., Mr. are you alright?" J.L. could hear it but something was again at his arm. But his first reaction was to swing wildly at the noise. Fortunately he missed and just whipped the air. He opened his eyes to notice a young bearded man near him with a look of concern on his face.

"Uh, yeah, I think so, 'cept my arm, a wolf bit me."

"That's what I'm trying to get a look at."

"Oh", J.L. stopped and let the young man look.

"Punctures, yes, but no ripped skin. Big though, and you think it was a wolf?"

"I couldn't see much in the night but that would be my guess." J.L. was now trying to rise and see just who was there.

"Molly", the young man called out, "Bring my bag would you?"

J.L. turned to look toward the young man who had hollered out.

He saw a small Conestoga wagon, blue with red wheels, and a dainty young woman stepping down. There were two small girls sitting up in the seat.

"Seth, I'm coming. Girls you stay here."

"Are you a doctor?" J.L. asked

"Will be, soon as we get to where we are going and I set up practice," said the man as he cleaned the wound, put a salve and bandaged his wrist. "How does that feel?"

"Like my arm's been wrenched a bit but I'll be okay. I guess I lucked out."

"Where did you folks come from?" J.L. asked.

"Actually we were just over the hill from you. Heard the rifle last night but didn't think we would move - little girls and all, until morning."

"Any sign of a dead wolf?"

"No, but saw some blood droplets off to the right."

Meanwhile Goliath was introducing himself to the little girls who had managed to come down from the wagon against their mother's wishes. He soon had them giggling as he gave some very wet kisses.

"We haven't had breakfast yet, would you join us?

"Let's make it a potluck." Said J.L. as he got the fire going, embers were still hot so it didn't take long and soon he had the coffee going.

Molly was soon busy with flap jacks and between what J.L. could provide, they all had a substantial breakfast. Turned out that this young family from Pennsylvania, were on their way to Pendleton first but then down to central Oregon, John Day or perhaps a place known as Deschutes or Riverbend.

During the breakfast the oldest girl, although no more than four, kept looking at J.L. "Mister, you look like a bear, a wooly old bear."

J.L. gave a little growl and the little girls squealed.

With traveling time being of the essence soon farewells and goodbyes were said and J.L. was off to the East and these kind folks off to the west. Those little girls warmed a place in his heart and evidently Goliath too.

J.L. made LaGrande that day, found a bath house and a boarding house and enjoyed the simple pleasures of food and rest for a night and hopefully looking something a little less than an ole bear. Goliath and Gus made do with a stable. Then he moved on to Baker City which meant one night out and then in town again where he sought the same. Here, at the mercantile, he stocked up as well as he could. He asked about what might be in the Snake River canyon as far as a town and told there was a place called Oxbow that provided some to the few adventurous who were trying to make life farming, ranching or hoping for ore in this formidable place. In asking he found that he could follow the Powder River most of the way but in the Halfway valley he would have to go over a mountain to get to Oxbow. He could follow the creek that drained down and that would take him to his destination.

The next morning was sunny and bright and getting hot quick, the three climbed the hills east of Baker, above the Powder. From there what J.L. saw struck him with awe. It seemed as if all he could see was endless barren mountains valleys that hid a mighty river in their midst somewhere.

Chapter Five
No Easy Time

*"For the Lord shall by thy confidence,
and shall keep thy foot from being taken."*
Proverbs 3:26

During the first night of J.L.'s trip over the Blues and Maddie's first night at a hotel, in a quiet way station a meeting took place. It was similar to one not too long ago. There was an angry little man and an apologetic, if he could actually get to that point, Clint Jeffers. Rather than a well appointed room, the two talked some 100 paces from the station in a shadowy place.

"He is heading towards the Snake River, some big canyon, looking for the son of the preacher you killed. And you are going to find him and that canyon or that river is a good place for him to finish his days and my misery." The old man stated.

"You want me to go there? I don't even know where that place is," Jeffers blustered.

"Out of Baker City, you can get directions. He is two days ahead of you but once in the canyon, he will be nosing around and you should be able to catch up with him there."

Jeffers started to protest until the man took five one hundred dollars bills out of his coat pocket and handed them to him.

"Get the job done and I will provide you twice this and then you and I can part company for good. But my patience is wearing thin with you. How could you miss him in Goldendale?"

Jeffers started to put up his bum hand.

"I know, don't show me it. Is it better?"

"Not much, pain is gone but it feels pretty useless but mark my word, I will get this done. The pain and misery he got me and this bum hand is worth it."

"That is a thousand dollars I have paid you so far, but there will not be another penny until you've done the job and bring me proof that he is dead and gone. Are we clear?"

~~~

Maddie was in the second day of her journey. She was anxious to get home and had felt she had been gone forever. But she occupied her time with helping her riding companion with the child. The older man that seemed to have so many questions yesterday was cordial today but was preoccupied with a book and watching the scenery.

~~~

After two days of travel over many a colorful, but barren hill and trying to follow the river, J.L. finally climbed high above the river. At the top of this ridge a beautiful valley lie before him. It looked like a place that would be good to ranch and farm, where grass and cattle would grow. To the North at the end of the valley were a beautiful set of mountains. He thought these might be called the Wallowa Mountains. There was still some snow on the highest of the peaks. As he rode into the valley he noticed that there were a few, very few, houses and ranches along the road. He was guessing now that he was at least halfway to the Snake River. As he rode closer to a settlement, just a couple of buildings was all, an older gent in a wagon was approaching the other way.

J.L. stopped and putting his hand up to signal that he hoped the wagon would stop. The older man did,

"Howdy, young fella, don't think I have seen you before," he said.

"Nope, first time."

"Are you coming here 'cause it doesn't look like you are equipped for mining in the canyon?"

"No not here just passing through but no, not mining. On an errand and I am heading for the Snake River," J.L. answered.

"Most young men I see heading that way, mind you, not many, are looking to strike it rich. Don't know if it will happen though, tough down there."

"Well, how much farther is 'down there'? I was hoping to be halfway by now," Said J.L.

"Interesting that you should say that, young fella, cause that is what we are a calling this place, Halfway."

"So, I am half way then?" asked J.L.

"Nope." Said the man matter of factly.

"Nope?"

"You are about two thirds of the way. Another day and you should run right into it, but you will probably want to go over that hill yonder then follow the creek down," The old man pointed to a huge hill to the Northeast.

"Where will that put me?"

"A place called Oxbow, where the river makes a big S turn. That seems to be a starting point for them boys who are looking for ore."

"So I am more than halfway yet you say they call this place, Halfway?"

"Yep, you can't name a place, two thirds, for crying out loud. What kind of name would that be?" The older gentlemen seemed to be actually irritated about the question.

"Halfway, now that has a ring to it. Anyway, good luck to you. You might look up Andy Culver down that way, he might be of a help to you. He's got a place a mile or so up river from Oxbow."

"Thanks Mister, and even though this is Halfway, I sure am glad I am two thirds of the way," J.L. said with a chuckle. He couldn't tell if the other fellow found that amusing as he was heading away, muttering to himself. 'God sure put some interesting folks on this green earth,' J.L. said to himself.

It was still early in the day so man, horse and dog took to the hill, zigzagging up its steep side on a trail that was barely scratched out. Once to the top, they rested and ate. There was plenty of grass on the downside. The trip down was sheer pleasure and soon they found the creek that the halfway fellow had mentioned. J.L. decided to get in a couple more hours and didn't stop until the sun sank low. The water was sweet and cool, and they found a good place to camp beneath ponderosa and willow.

The next morning J.L. was up early, coaxing Goliath to get moving. They continued to travel down. But they didn't see a soul. Finally, after wondering if these hills and valleys went on forever, J.L. rounded a bend and found that he was staring at a big, wild river below.

It was huge, like the Columbia but in this section, wild looking and set deep down. At the same time he needed to crane his head and neck way back to see the top of the mountains above. He thought it intriguing to see something so deep and yet so tall. The river just did like its namesake, twisted and turned like a snake. He could see off to his right the area of the river that looked like an oxbow, as the river serpentined through the rocks.

Looking to the North all he could see what looked like more endless mountains that held this great confluence of water. Once he arrived, now late afternoon, it was hot as could be. He estimated over the one hundred degree mark. He could understand why some called this place Hells Canyon cause that's sure what it felt like with the devil stoking this infernal.

He thought the sun should have seemed far away but it baked the canyon like an oven. Goliath and Gus both were heavy in perspiration. It was time to get them to water for a long cool drink and a soak.

He followed the river bend along a bit, now heading north and down stream, until he found a sandy area and easy descent.

At this point Goliath was in the water up to his chest, lapping great amounts of water and now and then, soaking in his whole head. Gus stood deep as well nearly to the bridle, he too, drank deeply. J.L. figured these guys knew what they were doing but unlike them, and no one around, he soon doffed his duds save for skivvies and was in the water. It was surprisingly cold but what relief. He paddled about, whooped a little as he went under and drank of the sweet water. They stayed for some while. J.L. wasn't happy to get out until he felt some numbing in his muscles and bones, the long ride this past week or so, had been murder on the old injury. He had learned long ago that nothing like a soak in cold water eased the pain.

After taking off Gus' saddle, reins and then hobbling the horse, he stretched out on his bedroll, didn't sleep although dozing did come and go. He just marveled at this incredible place. Like the Painted Hills, some months ago, he realized there was probably no place on God's green earth quite like this. 'Well, there was no God like the One he was learning about either.' He surmised.

"Spectacular", Maddie would have said and at that moment he so wished for she and Jacob to be here with him. It would be something to share this place and there was something about arriving at his destination that made him long for home. He had been so focused on this that he hadn't give home lots of thought, except at night before he nodded off and looked for the big dipper as Maddie had suggested. In his mind's eye he could see the two of them, Maddie and Jacob, splashing around in the water.

J.L. thought he might just spend the night here. And he wondered about catching a fish for dinner. As he looked around, hot as it was, he was pleased to see that many trees, bushes, wild flowers and sweet grass grew in abundance close to the river.

The sun had dipped enough that on the Idaho side, shadows began to grow up the sides of the canyon. He set to get his fishing gear, simple as it was, when he noticed a young man on horse back approaching from the south. J.L. gave a holler, "Howdy". Then thinking, as the man approached, maybe I need to be more presentable and went to pull on his britches.

"Howdy yourself, looks like you discovered the best place to be on this hot day." The man speaking was young and wiry and dressed like a farmer.

"You wouldn't happen to be Mr. Andy Culver* would you?"

*Andy Culver was one of the first settlers to make a home and living in Hells Canyon

"Yep, that would be me and how did you know?" he asked while taking off his hat and wiping the sweat from his brow with a handkerchief.

Talked to a fellow back in a well he called it Halfway even though it wasn't."

Are you a lookin' for me specific?" Andy asked.

"Sorta, looking for another fellow and was hoping you might have seen him."

"Not a lot of folks here and I don't know if I see 'em all but maybe. But I need to be getting back, livestock to feed before the sun sets but you are welcome to come along and share supper and I bet I can find a place for you and your dog to sleep."

"Thanks, much appreciated" J.L. said as he began to saddle Gus so as not to keep Andy waiting. Soon they were on their way the mile or two to his place. The canyon opened up to them as they rode along. Here and there, creeks, still flowing from the spring rains, ran into the huge river. The place was a jumble of boulders and vegetation that had found its way to the bottom of the canyon. J.L. noted a flock of wild turkeys and a couple small herds of Mule deer, mostly does and some fawns. High up on the sides of the canyon he could make out white splotches of something moving, he guess Big Horn sheep. He even noticed a larger black object high up but it moved into the shadows. This seemed to be a place for all of God's creatures. They seemed to use the steep walls as a step ladder to get to where the food was. He would plan to take a turkey or two if he could. And he wondered about the fishing. He imagined in his mind that Gideon would have been thrilled to try his chances on this river.

As they rode into Andy's compound, it was a pretty simple place. The ranch consisted of a small cabin, some out buildings, corrals, fences, fields that had been planted. A lot of work for one fellow but Andy seemed the type that had a boundless energy that kept him going from before dawn to after sunset. J.L. helped Andy as he could to finish up the day.

Afterwards it was beefsteak, pounded hard and cooked in lard and flour and some potatoes. But it seemed like ambrosia to J.L. After they were finished he produced the photo of the man he was looking for and shared a bit of the story of why he was looking. This seemed to perk up Andy's interest.

"You know, I pretty much stay to myself out here, it's what I like. Although a fair haired maiden looking for a hermit would be nice, so I don't really notice the folks that are coming in and out. Mind you it's not a lot although more than when I got here. Best I can suggest is that I will take you down river to my other place. Hardly a place at all but there is a little cabin there and you might use that as your HQ. I think if you are going to find this fella, it will be down river."

J.L. curled up on the floor for a while Goliath by his side but it was a bit too warm. So he headed outdoors and found a grassy spot under a tree. The moon was out, nearly full and the canyon was lit in eerily light. "What a place." He thought. He just marveled out God's creation. He thought himself most fortunate to live where he did but to see places like the Painted Hills, the Blues, the Wallowas and now this, well it just took the words and your breath away. Some came to these places to enjoy what God had provided and others seemed to just want to exploit creation for what they could get from it. Andy struck him as a fella that lived close to the earth, enjoyed its bounty, put up with its hardships and in a quiet way celebrated what God had provided.

This surmising didn't last long and soon he, and Goliath, head on his chest were out. They did not wake until sun rays over the eastern rim shown in their faces. Andy was already up and attending to some morning chores in the barn. J.L. could smell coffee and was glad to get that first cup.

About mid morning, after more chores and breakfast Andy and J.L. set out down river for the cabin. Along the way, in one canyon, where a good sized creek ran, a few men where working a new mind. The two of them stopped to chat and to inquire. But these boys were pretty much about their business and offered minimum hospitality and no help.

A couple of more hours passed by and after a trip over some ridges and edges that took your breath away and places where you could only walk not ride, they arrived at a small clearing along a heavily vegetated stream. Back amongst this was a small cabin, no more than 10 to 12 feet square in size.

"I staked this area as a claim, don't know if there is ore here but there is good water and you follow the stream and it opens up into a wide area full of trees. Well, it seemed a good place to plant an orchard or, well I don't know but it looks a bit of heaven" Andy explained.

Andy planned to stay the night; there were some things he wanted to do up the side canyon they were in.

The day had been hot and after Andy left, the cool water of the river beckoned beyond J.L.'s ability to resist and soon he and Goliath were in the cool water. There was a nice eddy at the stream mouth and it made for a good soaking spot. As he swam he noticed flashes of color and soon realized that dinner just had to be something with fins and a tail.

He was back out of the water, dressed only in his long handles, and with pole in hand he went back to the eddy, making short casts to the far side of it. As the river swirled his line moved and before long, BAM, a trout hit. It broke surface, flashed its writhing body and dipped back, heading for the deep. J.L. held on tight to the pole and after a bit of a fight landed a fat one, at least 18" long. He figured where there was one, there might be two. Sure enough, in no time, he extracted another one. He started a small fire, cleaned the fish and mounted them on diagonal sticks close to the fire. It made a fine dinner with some rough biscuits, a little dried fruit and some mustard tasting greens he found. Maddie had picked this before, many times, and so while J.L. knew little about this kind of gathering, he was sure this would be okay. It was, a bit of a bite to it but it just seemed to add to the dinner.

Again rather than stay in the cabin J.L and Andy found soft spots under a tree to call their beds. J.L. slept like he was dead and, again, the sun was in his face before he rose.

~~~

Clint Jeffers, on that very day, rode into that place called Halfway. He came in early evening, it was his way. The sneaky life that he lived caused him to think about traveling and being around others as being kept to a minimum. Tonight, though, he hoped for two things, a few cold beers and some idea about just where he was. This place wasn't really a town so much but there was a saloon on the edge of the most populated area. There were a couple of horses out front and an old wagon. Not much in the way of humanity, he thinking that most of the cowpokes that came to wet their whistle were already back at the ranch and in the bunk house.

The place was dark but fairly cool compared to the heat outside. It had been a hot crossing the last couple of days even with staying in the shade and resting most of the day. Jeffers pulled up to the bar, dropped a few coins and hollered out "Get a beer here?" to no one in particular. There was no one behind the bar. A couple of ranch hands sat at a table far in a corner, an older man was bellied up near the other end.

"Sure, sure, keep your shirt on." a voice came from nowhere to be seen but soon a portly man with a thick mustache and mutton chops appeared from what must be a little office or kitchen towards the back but Clint was not sure. "Actually, a day like this probably wouldn't mind having the shirt off. Hot enough for you fella?" the bartender said as he poured a tall mug of amber liquid.

Clint just grunted a 'huh uh' back and took to the beer downing most of the mug in one gulp. "I'll have another, while you are close to that tap. And how about some grub, got anything?"

"Sure fella, got some ham and cheese and the Missus baked fresh loves of bread just today. I'll be right back, one or two for you."

"Make it two"

The older gent at the other end kind of sidled down towards Jeffers looking to make conversation. He could have cared less except to find out where he was and how close to the Snake River.

"Hotter than blazes out there today, hey?" the old man started.

"Yep."

"Don't think I've seen your face about here afore."

"Nope, just passing through and where is this?" Clint was conscious of his deformed hand, which he now kept in a glove, except at night unless it was cold. He still couldn't do much with it but the pain was gone so he guessed it might make a good club if needed.

"Well, you are in Halfway, least that's what some of us call it."

"Halfway, like in halfway from Baker to the Snake River Canyon?"

"Yes and no", the old fellow smiled, thinking 'here is another one in just the last couple of days trying to get to that insufferable canyon.

Jeffers gave the old man a hard look that said he wasn't in the mood for funnin'

"Better than that", the man stammered a bit. "Two thirds and another short day you can be there. That where you're a headed?"

"Yeah, looking for a fella. Big guy might be traveling with a dog."

The old man blurted out, "Yeah, talked with him yesterday or the day before." But there was something about the look in this hombre's face that made the man think that maybe that wasn't information to offer. But Jeffers said nothing and his face showed no emotion.

Clint had about finished the second mug and at that moment the bar tender appeared with sandwiches wrapped in paper.

"That'll be another two bits and it looks like you have it right here."

Jeffers grabbed up the food and turned to go, asking as he did, "Do I just follow that creek down to the canyon?"

"Yeah, sort of, you will need to go cross country a bit. The bartender said to Clint Jeffers back as he disappeared into the night.

Jeffers rode only far enough to get down by the creek, in a cool spot where the water was near. He decided to pass on a fire that night. He surely didn't need one to stay warm. There was some moon up that night so he could make out logs and rocks among the shadows. He laid out his bedroll on a little bluff of grass just above the creek. Then he stripped down to long handles and sat with feet in the water and ate the sandwich. Then he splashed water on to his head and neck. He thought it felt as good as the best shot of whiskey money could by. He cupped his hands and drank some which helped to chase off the beer taste in his mouth which was for some reason bitter tonight.

There was something that was nagging at him that he quite couldn't get to. Kind of like an itch in the small of your back you can't reach or a little sliver you can spot but just seems to have away of annoying you all day.

Jeffers was a man who liked it easy. However he could make his keep, illegal more often than not, was fine by him. He had been that way along time, hard to remember when he wasn't although there was a time ... This whole business was becoming too much, he was not beginning to care so much for it. Matthews was a pain in the drawers. And he was not a forgiving kind so his ruined hand was always a reminder of what had happened. But there was also something going on that said, 'enough is enough'. He hoped to kill J.L. as soon as he could, collect his money and be on to other places, California maybe or even farther.

But if he didn't get his prey, soon, he was all for taking what he had and calling it quits.

~~~

On the next morning at the cabin J.L. and Andy were talking just before Andy headed back up the canyon.

"What's it like downriver and where might I be looking for miners?" J.L. asked

Andy answered the second part of the question first, "Could be about anywhere, but I would concentrate on the creeks that flow into the canyon. There are quite a bit of them though. But you could find some miners chopping away at a bank too but I would think you are most likely going to find him down around the mouth of the Imnaha River. Folks have been finding some ore in there."

"How far down in that?"

"Quite a ways, it will take you days to get there from this direction, 'specially if you are going to be checking every creek along the way. Most folks come over from LaGrande to Joseph and then to the Imnaha. It is shorter, no less easier though, but that may have saved you some time.

J.L. thanked Andy for his hospitality. He was invited back to his ranch at Oxbow anytime. "I hope you find your man and I hope the fella that might be looking for you ain't so lucky."

The next morning, before the sun was up, J.L. turned Gus' head north and down river. Goliath seemed ready to go and they headed out on the rough road. J.L. had no sense about how far he would try to get, just go until he was too tired to go anymore he figured.

As he rode on, the sun was breaking on the canyon walls, not much color yet because of the heat and no clouds, but soon the canyon walls were drenched in light. The sides of this canyon seemed to go up so far as to wonder just how far that might be. Could he be looking up a whole mile in some places he wondered? The whole place was so vast, just this little section looked formidable indeed. He took some comfort in knowing that others had found there way so perhaps it wasn't setting off only to find the end of the world and no way back.

He thought a bit about Andy and his desire to make a life for himself in such a place. Yep, it seemed like it could be hostile but yet, as last night they rested before turning, as serene as one would imagine heaven.

Then the conversation they had came up about how J.L. may have done better to have gone a different route. It was like God was now having a conversation with him. He now remembered that when he had the chance to consider the other routes he had a nagging feeling that he should have chose them. Just a feeling he guessed but a bible verse came to mind, perhaps something Maddie or the preacher had shared, something to do with the need to listen to the still small voice. In that God was there to direct but that one needed to being listening. Could this be, he thought, an example of this? Was that still small voice at those two points in the trip saying, "This way, this way."

He also recognized that while he was learning a bit about praying, talking to God mostly about Maddie, Jacob, help to find Joseph, that he may not be listening. Was prayer just a matter of requests and repentance or was it to be more of a conversation – two-way, each party listening. Something to think about, he thought. In this still place, except for the splash of river or creek running into it there was above all other things, a great silence. Perhaps a real opportunity to listen for that still small voice he thought.

J.L., horse and dog plodded on and there was no easy way after a while. You didn't just follow the river. There was ravine and bluff, out cropping, shale rock that wanted to slip out from under your feet and hollows all along the way. Up and down, back and forth, sometimes needing to walk and leading Gus over treacherous rock. He could just imagine getting to some point to discover there might be a place where it just didn't look like one could go farther. He wondered how much he might have to climb, that mile up. Could he wade Gus safely? Shallow spots were to be found but to him, it just looked like he was getting deeper into the canyon the farther he went.

There were sections he saw where the water ran frothy white like a mad dog against the rocks and other places so serene the desire to float upon it was almost unbearable to not do so on these blistering hot days.

On this first full day out he had not encountered one living human soul and little evidence that anybody had been here before. Shadows were beginning to grow long and the west side of the canyon was now fully engulfed in them. He found a small creek running into the river and headed down it until he reached the river. Here was a sandy bar that looked like an excellent place for a camp and even a cooling dip.

Hells Canyon

Unsaddled, Gus was up to his knees drinking deeply. Goliath did what any black hot canine would do on this day, dog paddle. Soon J.L. was in with a whoop. The water was cool and refreshing and surprising cold the deeper he went. As he did his own version of the dog paddle he noticed that he seemed to have company, flashes of sliver darted and brushed against his legs. This only meant one thing; fish would be a must on the menu tonight.

Back out he gathered up his fishing gear and soon caught a channel cat, a couple of pounds at least. Filleted out and on the fire it went real well with the biscuits and beans he had brought. Goliath settled for biscuits and jerky and there was plenty of sweet grass and wild flowers to keep Gus interested.

That night J.L. lay out under the stars. There was just a hint of a moon, but enough to reveal the shadows of steep cliffs rising above him, as he marveled at where he was. It gave him thought to once again considering how great God must be to make such a place. Just one place that held a thousand places on this home called Earth. He had seen drawings and read about Grand Canyon in the Arizona Territory and imagined that place must be no less astounding. At the same time he felt again a great sense of loneliness knowing that he was so far from Jacob and Maddie. He remembered that Maddie had said to him, "John, every night that I can I am going to go out and look at the stars above, maybe you might do the same thing. And even though we can't see each other, we'll be looking at the same stars at the same time and maybe we won't feel quite so far away from each other". J.L. thought that helped a bit, remembering that. He thought he might stare at those stars long into the night, off in the distance he could hear the howl of a coyote, but before he realized it, the sun was shining in his face and he could hear Goliath howling something terrible.

He got up quickly and headed towards the noise which was up in a draw. It seemed like Goliath was back behind a bunch of brush and plants he didn't recognize. He made his way behind them as quickly as he could and was surprised to notice a sharp jab in his leg. He thought maybe he'd been bitten by a snake, it hurt so much, but he did not see one. He could see the black form of Goliath up ahead of him and as he got close he saw the dog with his face up against the strange plant. From that plant spikes protruded and a half dozen of them stuck into Goliath's muzzle holding him fast. He tried to comfort the dog howling by stroking his neck carefully saying "easy boy, easy, easy". He knew he had to go back to his saddle bags, so retreated back carefully while watching for the spines in the plants. He found his tools he brought with him and once he got back to Goliath, he decided it made more sense to snip the barbs from the plant thus freeing Goliath. He did so as gingerly as possible as Goliath showed great patience with whining and whimpering.

Once that was done, J.L. led Goliath back down to the river, coaxing him into the cold water. He then would push Goliath's wounded inflamed muzzle into the water. Goliath would jump and try to pull back, JL kept at it until the dog seemed to realize the frigid water eased the pain some.

Now came the hard task. After he felt that Goliath's wounded muzzle was numbed enough by the water, he began to carefully pull out one of the spikes. After he'd gotten that first one out he realized that each barb had a curve to it, so slowly pulling down and out, he was able to get the remaining 10 barbs out. The process seemed to take forever. JL was amazed at how brave Goliath was and how much trust he had put in him throughout the entire ordeal. They returned to the river to repeat the dousing for a while longer. Then he led Goliath to a shady spot underneath a willow tree. He retrieved to salve from his saddle bags that Maddie had packed for him just in case he got injured himself. This he put on the wounds hoping the dog would not lick it right off. He didn't and was fine to just settle down to rest closing his eyes. JL didn't think Goliath slept because he could still hear him whimpering. He also knew there wouldn't be any travel this day.

After a short while, JL let Gus down to the stream for some water, then let him to a grassy area by the water and hobbled him close so that the horse, too, wouldn't wander into the same spiky plants. Now, he was ready to return and investigate the plant that had caused so much trouble. There was a small grove of them, he thought the plant looked strange but it might be something known as cactus he'd heard about. Each leaf was pear shaped and full of mean barbs. But there were red looking fruits on many of them that looked appetizing just seeming impossible to get to.

It was now well into the afternoon; J.L thought he would try his hand at fishing again and just make the best of the day and hopefully catch some dinner. He again had some luck, and as evening began to settle in, he enjoyed another repast of fish. He took Goliath down for water, but Goliath was not interested in eating anything. He felt blessed to have this big dog as his companion. That night sleep passed in a blur of wild dreams, mostly from his time in the War Between the States. But just before he woke up, he could feel this heaviness in his chest that he couldn't understand. He startled awake his eyes popping open only to see a heavy boot pressing heavily on his chest. As he adjusted his sight, he could see the barrel of a rifle. And just behind that, none other than Clint Jeffers.

He started to move, but Jeffers pressed even harder saying "Hold tight right there Mathews unless you want this to be your last minute." JL lay back thinking in that split moment 'What am I going to do'? At that moment, though, suddenly Goliath was there and he had a big bite of Clint Jeffers' back side, and was holding on. This was enough to cause Jeffers to lose his balance allowing J.L. to start for his feet. Jeffers swung wildly at the dog with the rifle but, cursing loudly.

He was able to hit the dog in the muzzle with the gun, Goliath yelped and retreated back a few feet. By this time J.L. was on his feet and lunging towards Jeffers. They began to grapple with each other in a violent bear hug, each man trying to pull the other one down and hitting with their fists. J.L. had camped on the edge of a rock that was set high above the river with rapids below and as the two men struggled, they unknowingly moved closer and closer to the edge. J.L. could hear Goliath begin to bark wildly and then all of a sudden Jeffers was hit from behind by a lunging Goliath. This force was powerful enough to send the two men over the edge and into the rocky rapids below.

Goliath kept his footing but looked down whimpering as his master and the bad man were being washed below. He ran down to the bank and into the water but turned back as he too began to get swept away in the white froth of the rapids.

The two men hit the water hard. There was a log in the water and J.L.'s head landed on it with a smack. This rendered him into a semi-conscious state.

The force of the landing of Jeffers on J.L. knocked the air out of him. He was not much of a swimmer anyway and now he was fighting for his breath and life as he pitched into the white froth doing all he could to keep his head up and trying to catch his breath.

He went under a few times, each time coming up and gurgling water. But he was able to latch on to a passing log with one arm. He drifted for some time, not quite able to get his breath back but finally he was able to pull into a rocking shore and lay upon the ground feeling like a drowned rat.

J.L., in his state, managed to move over on his back. Not that he was aware much but this kept him afloat and he floated for a long time, the rest of the day. Somewhere in this blurry journey he too was able to grab on to a log. For some time the log became tangled in some overhanging brush but J.L. was not aware enough to try to get to shore. He just simply hung on.

After a while the log came free and the journey continued until he floated into the eddy of a large stream flowing from the west side of the canyon.

He floated into plain view of some Chinese miners who were working a claim there. One miner swam out and pulled J.L. to the bank. It was difficult the man was quite small compared to J.L.'s bear of a size. Other hands reached out for him and drug him to shore.

As for Jeffers and after some time he mustered himself and began to rise. But as he stood he heard the sound of whooping near him. The sound he had heard before by natives on the war path. And that is exactly who was there, a few natives, in war paint who grabbed him up and drug him to the upper bank. One native, with a cruel look on his face, had pulled a large knife. Jeffers had no other thought than this was the end of him. His hope was that the natives would be quick in killing him but he feared this might not be the case. He was not a praying man by any degree but his thought was, 'What if there is heaven and hell? If such a thing existed he knew he was not heading to the Pearly Gate. The native had a hold of Jeffers head; he was doing all he could to flail about. He tried to shout at them but his voice was not there. He closed his eyes waiting for the inevitable but there was another voice, more seasoned than the others.

Jeffers opened his eyes to see an old man, but still strong, wrestling with the young buck and shouting in an authoritative manner. The young brave let go and Jeffers crumpled to the ground, still trying to catch his breath. He was shivering and shaking uncontrollably.

Whatever the old man said the young braves retreated and were soon mounted, whooping as they went.

The old man went off for a minute but reappeared with a blanket in which he covered Jeffers. He disappeared again this time returning with some sort of bitter tasting beverage. He encouraged Jeffers to drink it all by hand motions. Jeffers did and he was surprised how better he began to feel but he also felt tired and was soon asleep. When he awoke it was night. He could see the old man near a small fire. He went out again and the next time he woke it was a bright morning and the man was not to be found.

Jeffers decided that he wasn't too worse for wear for the experience. He needed to get back on the other side to find his horse. Then he would have to decide if he would continue is search for Matthews. He liked to believe that he was dead, drowned in the river. He had to hike a couple of miles back up river before he could find a placid area to swim across. Even as gentle as the water looked here the undercurrent was strong and the water cold but he made it across. He found his horse still hobbled where he left it.

He was up river about a quarter of a mile from where Matthews had been camped. He began to ride down river, quietly as he could until he could make out the ledge where the fight took place. No Matthews, he noticed but he could see the dog pacing on the cliff edge. He wasn't sure where the horse was. He thought about stealing the horse and belongings but second thought it and decided he didn't need a confrontation with the dog. He could always just shoot it but the reality was he had a belly full of the whole ordeal.

Matthews just didn't seem so important anymore. Collecting his money from the little man and high tailing it out of the Columbia River Gorge country seemed the best idea. Maybe he would head south or north but someplace else. He turned his horse's head and headed back up river and out of the canyon and hopefully out of this whole business altogether. He had a stray thought or two about the old native that saved his life. It was not something to be expected he thought and certainly nothing he would have done unless it was to his advantage and yet, well, he just didn't know but it was something for sure.

The next morning J.L. was feeling not so bad other than a king sized headache. He recalled being attended to during the night. Encouraged to drink some sort of soup and a tea he guessed. He recalled some small hands, could see them in his mind, attending to him. He thought they were small enough to be a child's yet were dainty and of a small woman he had to believe.

"You alright there Mr. San?" he heard somebody speak in broken English.

"A, yep, think so." J.L. rose up and looked for the voice he just heard. To his left and near a small fire three men sat eating breakfast he assumed.

"What day and time is it?"

"A, not so sure on the day but it is morning. Are you hungry?" one of the men asked.

"Yep, believe so."

"How you feel?" asked the same man.

"Well, I think alright, not so bad actually considered I must have floated for some time. Do you know what part of the river we are on?"

"Imnaha." The man said.

At the rivers mouth, J.L. thought. This was his hoped for destination, where he thought he might find Joseph.

J.L. rose to his feet and walked the few feet to the little fire and sat back down. "I can't thank you enough for saving me."

"What you doing anyway, in that river?" said the same little man with broken English.

J.L. told them his story. The man translated it to the other two. J.L. noticed what seemed to be a sigh of relief from them. Evidently he was now not considered a threat. Then J.L. asked, "Wasn't there a woman or a girl too?"

The English speaking man sat quiet for a minute obviously deep in thought. "Uh, we a scared for her, keep her hid away. There are other mens who would want her . . . maybe hurt her. You know?"

"Yep, sure do, but you are all safe with me. I would just like to thank her."

The man, named Chang, as J.L. found out, hollered out but not loudly, "Mai Lee."

Soon a little woman appeared from the brush. She was quite small and J.L. figured she could probably hide behind a big leaf. He rose to meet her only to notice her trying to shrink from. He immediately sat back down. "I just wanted to say thank-you Ma'am for your kindness.

Mai Lee understood English and she nodded and said, "You are welcome." She then joined the others by the fire for a few minutes but saying nothing. J.L asked Chang how it was going with the mining and got a miner's answer back; vague not wanting to let on if they were finding ore.

J.L. offered, "I would be honored to help you today if you are going to do some mining. I am big and strong . . ."

Chang appraised him up and down then spoke to the others who all soon gave a hearty nod. That seemed to be an invitation to Mai Lee who started getting breakfast. It was quite simple, some rice, some wild berries she had found and some roots that didn't look too appetizing. J.L., who was hungry, as can be refrained himself.

J.L. got his wish and more with the offer to help. In fact he felt most like a pack mule and he hauled sand, rock, ore and anything else the men wanted done. Mai Lee mostly stayed out of the way and mostly up creek doing he didn't know what.

The day went on until long shadows crept up the canyon walls and the most appetizing aroma came from the little campfire.

Supper never tasted so good, hot succulent and plenty, he was three plate full in before he began to get filled. He decided not to ask what the meal was, the rice he recognized, and some sort of meat and some other things he was not so sure on. But it didn't matter it was just too good.

J.L. headed out early, at first light. His hope was to get back to his camp by the end of the day. He also realized that may be a bit much in asking. And it was. Traversing the canyon meant up and down and in and out. Clamoring over sharp cliffs, hiking up steep steams, sometimes fording through the waters and mostly following deer trails that often seem to stop with nowhere to turn but back.

He believed that he would know where he was in relationship to the cliffs above and that he might actually recognize where he had camped. He had taken special interest in his surroundings so as to have a better sense.

The shadows were now beginning to grow long and he was very tired. It had been at least 12 hours of hiking through the most difficult terrain he had ever been in. he found a place that offered a bit of a clear and sandy area where he could settle down for the night. After eating his sparse meal and drank what seemed like a gallon or two of the river. He decided to pass of building a fire as it certainly wasn't cold, in fact he was covered in sweat and he soon was down to nothing more than his smile on and in the refreshing water.

He soaked for a long time, his back was really hurting him, and if he could have figured out a way to have slept in the water for the night, he would have. After a long time in the water and feeling quite numb from the cold, he reveled at how quickly he dried off in the hot breezy weather. He had no bedroll but as it was he was becoming very sleepy. He managed to pull on his long handles and fell asleep with his arm as his pillow. He slept long and hard and woke with a start and the bright sun in his eyes. He had no idea of what time it was, but thought it might be later than he'd hoped. After eating the remainder of his meager supplies, he headed out again.

He traveled a few hours and it was already becoming very hot, but the cliffs on the Idaho side began to look familiar to him, and he believed he was close. He began to shout out "Goliath, Goliath!" every now and then, but there was no response. He continued on trying not to lose hope and believing that his horse and dog were still safe. He called out again and was encouraged more than he could imagine by the response of a familiar bark. Soon he heard a crashing sound through the brush, like a grizzly bear beginning to spring, and suddenly there was Goliath…mid air…landing on J.L. and his tongue lapping at his face.

The dog and he rolled around in joyful abandon for a moment until J.L. pushed him off saying "Where's Gus boy, where's Gus?" Goliath immediately turned tail and headed back through the brush and led J.L. to a tangled briar where Gus had managed to get himself into. J.L. said "Hold on boy, I'll get you out" and was pleased to find his saddle, saddlebags and blanket right where he'd left them, undisturbed.

Once again, He retrieved his tool that he had used to extract the cactus barbs from Goliath. Using it, he cut away at the briars to free Gus. The horse was a bit scratched up, but really no worse for wear. J.L. decided to spend the rest of the day and night there, he was hungry and imagined the dog was too. But instead of fishing he hoped for some game. He had seen some turkey and rabbit earlier and thought that if maybe he could get Goliath to settle down and hide quietly in the brush that perhaps the Lord would bless them with a fine meal. As both man and dog waited sleep came and they napped in the shade of the hot afternoon. But as he awoke, as if the Lord had heard his prayer, a covey of quail came into view. He raised he rifle and was able to bag a couple before the rest of the frightened birds skittered away.

Hells Canyon

It wasn't a lot, but it would tide him and the dog over until something else would become available. The next morning they all headed out back down the canyon. J.L. didn't think he was in such a hurry but he felt a compelling force to move on travelling all day long. That evening he was able to bag two rabbits, making a much more substantial meal. It was just as difficult going back, at times he was able to ride Gus, more often than not, he had to lead the horse through every kind of imaginable terrain. The day was growing long and he was beginning to wonder if they would make it back to the Chinamen's miner's camp that night.

He didn't really think it mattered but he figured they may have a good meal for him that would be better that what he would find on the trail. And again there was this compelling sense to get back as soon as possible. As he rode over the next hill and down into a little valley he realized that he had entered into the river basin where the miner's camp was. In the twilight he could see a fire ahead of him about two hundred yards but instead of just three of four Chinese miners he could see three other larger men. There was a commotion going on and as he carefully approached he could see that one of the men was holding Chang with what looked like a gun to his throat. The two other men had a hold of May Lai. The man that had Chang was shouting loudly, but J.L. could not quite make out the words.

He then noticed that the man let go of Chang, Chang moved back towards his partners and motioned to them and the three lay on the ground. Nearby were three horses and the men mounted them, one of them throwing May Lee over the saddle like a bag of feed. They soon took off across the river. J.L. could only imagine the worse. He decided to pursue them, drawing his rifle. Goliath had the same idea but was ahead of J.L. already heading across the river in pursuit. As J.L. got mid stream the three men were on the other bank and were already dismounted. Goliath was barking madly and had just come out of the water, three men looked up seeing Goliath and J.L., and drew their guns.

One man fired not at J.L. but at Goliath, a bullet ricocheting nearby. J.L. felt he had no other choice, with rifle in hand he fired a shot at him. The bullet hit the man in mid section and he crumpled. The two other men had begun to fire also. J.L. stopped Gus short, jumping from the horse. As soon as he landed he raised his rifle and took aim, firing off a few more shots. And soon the other two men lay on ground with their partner.

J.L. looked at a moment at the three still bodies, shaking his head. He would have done anything to have avoided killing these men. He rode back across the river, coaxing Goliath with him. He asked about a shovel. Chang found two, mounted up on the back of Gus with J.L. and they headed back across the river.

The two dragged the bodies of the three up off the bank and into a sandy hollow. They dug graves and placed the three in it. They were both silent during the grim job. J.L. thought about making crosses or markers and whether he should say some words but, somehow, the thought had no appeal. That feeling also stuck in his craw too. The whole business was just too much.

J.L. let Chang ride Gus back. He wanted to take a long dunk in the river and see if he could wash all of this away. The cool water in the moonlight felt refreshing and cleansing. Goliath decided to swim with J.L. Soon he was splashing around him as if to play. The man and the dog tussled in the water until both were soaked good.

When J.L. climbed, out Mai Lee was waiting with towels to dry them off. He then slipped behind the bushes, disrobed, dried and dressed with clothes he had fetched from his saddle bags.

Mai Lee spent some time tending to Goliath, almost as if she was in no hurry for the task to end. 'Something else to think about.' thought J.L.

He settled down by the fire with the three other men. Mai Lee joined them and cuddled close to J.L. like a daughter might do to her father. J.L. didn't really know what to think but involuntarily put his big arm around her. She laid her small head on his chest and soon began to weep quietly.

That prompted the men to talk among themselves. A minute later Chang spoke up. "I think we would all be dead if it were not for you," he said, directing his comment at J.L.

"Huh?" said J.L., pondering it through.

"I think when they got done with Mai Lee, we'd be killed. Many miners, here, hate us Chinese."

J.L. had certainly seen this kind of attitude of hatred directed at other Orientals before. It was not what he and Maddie thought by any means. It was hard for him to fathom such contempt for this group of people. For the most part they were hard working people who kept to themselves. And has he had said to Maddie and Jacob before, 'We all came from someplace else.

"You fellas will need to be extra careful now. And I would say that it would be a good idea to get Mai Lee out of here." Perhaps there was a safer place, but perhaps not, J.L. languished in the thought.

Mai Lee had stopped crying but was now softly humming, barely over a whisper. She seemed to have no plans to leave J.L.'s side. The little tune was unrecognizable to him but pleasant in a sad way. He was so tired, though, after these days in the canyon he was soon asleep.

Once asleep it seemed as if in no time at all he was back into the war, reliving another part of it but with all the bizarreness of the stuff of dreams. This time was later than the battle that had left him wounded and clinging to life for some months following. Now he was south of there and at Andersonville Prison. He was not a prisoner. This was an infamous facility that housed union soldiers. Because of J.L.'s further need for convalesce but also because of his size he had been reassigned as a prison guard to this horrible place. He had traveled by train, in a box car and was now assigned a duty he would never have imagined or desired. It was a place of death and despair.

Somewhere in the night the comforted became the comforter. As J.L. was dreaming, reliving and now struggling in his sleep a little hand with a damp cloth wiped his face and brow. She spoke soft Chinese words and after a while J.L. just slept without the nightmares.

Chapter Six
Final Hours

*"Wherefore should I fear in the days of evil,
when the iniquity of my heels shall compass me about?"*
Psalm 49:5

After another day with the Chinese miners, J.L. headed north and down river again. He was only into his trek and hour or so when he came upon another miner's camp. At first he didn't see anyone around and wondered if the camp was abandoned. Everything looked in disarray. As he rode into camp and began to dismount an old man with wild hair and a disheveled appearance appeared from the shadow of a rock cliff. The man had a rifle up and started shouting, "Back off stranger or lead will fly and you will die."

"Hold up ole timer, I am not here to harm or rob you just looking for a friend of mine." J.L. stood frozen with a big hand on Goliath.

"Who you be lookin' for but I probably ain't seen him. Don't see much of anybody and that suits me fine," the old man replied.

"The fella's name is Joseph Gideon." J.L. stated.

"Nope, don't know him so you just get back on your horse and you and that dog high tail it out." The man now had his rifle raised. Goliath had begun to growl. J.L. was trying to shush him quietly. He also felt like this was not true. He didn't know why so he figured he would bluff a bit. "Are you sure, there is a reward from his family. Maybe you didn't hear me right," J.L. said and then repeated the name again. "Joseph Gideon, tall fella, probably in his 40's."

"Reward?" said the old man. "Did you say Joe Gideon? My hearing ain't what it used to be."

"Yeah, brothers and sisters are real worried about him. My name is J.L. Matthews and they asked me to find him. What be your name, Sir?"

"Pitts, not spits but pits. Justin Pitts, everyone calls me Just Pitts, drat them," said Pitts, as if he was spitting.

"Nice to meet you, Mr. Pitts."

"Well, I got work to do but that fella was my partner for a time. But he left. And I need me a partner, ain't getting any younger."

"Um, maybe I could help you," said J.L. trying to buy a little time.

"No, Sir, you just stay where you're at. Although a little filly that didn't talk too much would be good," the man said with a little nasty chuckle in his voice.

"When did he leave?" J.L. said feeling a bit of excitement.

"I don't know, just a little while ago. Said he was sick. I think maybe he's got the consumption."

"A little bit ago, like today?" J.L. could feel his heart climb into his throat.

"Well, no, not today but, well a couple a days, maybe a week."

J.L.'s heart now sunk. If it had truly been a few days then he really did just miss him. Taking the wrong road, the attack by Jeffers, the incident with the Chinese miners; all this weighed heavy on him. If none of this had happened this way he may have made it in time. He wanted to yell at the sky like that might do some good.

After a bit J.L. asked, "Where was he going?"

The old man had turned to walk back into the tunnel.

"I don't know, mister, maybe Baker City, or I think, maybe Canyon City."

Without a word, his mood dark, J.L. was back on his horse and turning to leave.

"Hey, didn't you say something about a reward?" The old man hollered from the dark mine shaft.

"Yeah, if we find him," J.L. shouted back, with a guilty feeling of pleasure knowing the old man wouldn't get a red cent from him today.

"Get out here, you --- afore I start to shooting. You are all the same just after what you can get."

J.L. didn't need another invite and headed back across the creek and glad to disappear in a grove of willow and elderberry trees.

He felt like swearing but didn't. He sure wanted to yell at something but what. All he wanted to do now was just get out of this insufferable canyon as quickly as he could. That would be a couple of days at least. He started back up the canyon. Stopping briefly to once again thank the Chinese miners that helped him and let them know he had found out what he needed. He cautioned them to be really careful, that even though this was supposed to be a free country for all, that maybe being here wasn't such a good idea. He liked to think that their problems were over with those three scoundrels gone but he knew that might not be the case.

It took him two days and nights to reach the Oxbow area and he was once again welcomed by Andy who seemed glad for the company. J.L. rode in during the middle of the afternoon, when the canyon was at its hottest. It was a good time for a soak in the river and a nap on Andy's porch. That evening he helped Andy with a project that took them to nearly midnight to finish. J.L. stayed another day and then the next morning after that set out of the canyon.

A mile out and up he rode to top of a hill to get a last glimpse of this incredible but hostile place. His feelings were mixed. He thought no place was more incredible on the face of the earth. He thought that way about The Painted Hills too. He decided you couldn't compare; both just as grand and just as different. It would have been nice to see it under different circumstances. He wondered if he would ever be back. There was a feeling if not, oh well, yet the desire to show this to Maddie and Jacob. These were all thoughts for another time, as he turned Gus' head towards the west.

Three more days and he was in Baker City. He found the telegraph office and wired Maddie his whereabouts and his plans. His hope was that maybe after a long week he might be home. And his thoughts were that it would be a long time before he was willing to leave his place along the Chenoweth Creek.

He spent a full day nosing around town to see if there were neither hide nor hair of Joseph; there wasn't.

A few more days of travel through country he had never seen before and he arrived in Canyon City. He rode in at the noon hour, hungry and thirsty. The urge for food was strong but the urge for a few beers to wash it down with was even stronger. This thought weighed heavy on him and caused him quite a quandary. He found a stable for Gus and the man who ran it was glad to take Goliath for a while and see him well fed for a nominal price. J.L. then headed across to the nearest hotel, this sat next to a saloon. He forced himself to the hotel first but his mind was on the swinging saloon doors and the cool place inside. He could imagine a few sandwiches, some pickled eggs and few beers bellied up to the bar.

As he stepped into the shadow of the board walk and reached for the door, it swung open before he had a chance to grab the knob. The form of a woman was coming through. He jumped back, she seemed intent on getting through the door but was looking back and thanking somebody for something.

He started out, "Scuse me Ma'am ... a ... I mean Maddie. Maddie!" It was Maddie coming through the door and she pretty much ran head long into him.

"Oh, John!" she exclaimed. "I have been looking for you since yesterday, hoping I didn't miss you."

"Miss me, why are you here? Oh, but I am so glad to see you . . . but . . ."

Maddie reached out for him, putting her arms around. "Give us a kiss first and then I will explain."

Maddie took John to a nice café down the street and away from the temptation of the saloon. During bites of a big meal for him and a bit for Maddie, which she just picked at, they both caught each other up.

"So you came thinking that maybe you would get here before me and find Joseph?"

"Yes, and I did!" she said with excitement. "He is staying at a boarding house just at the edge of town. I stayed there last night too. But he is very ill. Mrs. Hudson thinks he might die."

"What's wrong with him? His partner thought he had the consumption."

"No, no it is not that. The doctor who has seen him doesn't know what is wrong with him but thinks it is very peculiar maybe even suspicious."

"What's this?"

"When we get back to the rooming house we will talk with Mrs. Hudson. And I think she will let us talk with him when she knows you are here."

"So you have not talked with him?"

"No, I thought I would wait a bit, hoping you would arrive in time."

Maddie and J.L. walked a quarter of a mile to the neat and freshly painted two story house. It had a bit of a Cape Cod look to it and J.L. thought it might have been a kit house from back east. Mrs. Hudson, a neat, plump woman of advancing age was in the parlor sewing.

"Mrs. Hudson, look who I found!" Maddie said excitedly.

"The Mister I imagine." Said she, rising and extending a dainty but weathered hand.

"Pleased to meet you, Ma'am."

They all talked pleasantries for a few minutes and then Maddie asked about Joseph.

"Dr. Turner was here just a bit ago. He is very concerned and doesn't think Mr. Thomas is long for this plain."

"Is is possible for us to see him?" J.L. asked, "We have some important things to tell him."

"I think so, he sleeps much but when he is awake, he is quite lucid. Seems to understand what is happening to him."

Mrs. Hudson ushered them into a dark, cool room. A still form lay on the bed. At first J.L. thought, 'We are too late."

"Mr. Thomas, it's me, Mrs. Hudson. I have brought some nice people who need to talk to you."

A voice coming from the bed said something weakly that was not to be understood.

"Mr. Thomas, this is John and Maddie. They are from The Dalles and they know your family over in Goldendale. They have some important things to tell you," Mrs. Hudson persisted and speaking in a louder voice.

"From Goldendale?" The voice trailed off.

Mrs. Hudson opened some curtains in the room and light filled in. J.L. could now see the man clearly. He looked much like Gideon only younger and looking very poorly. Mrs. Hudson approached him in tenderly fashion asking "Are you feeling well enough for visitors Joseph"? He replied back, yes, that he was. J.L. and Maddie approached the bed and Mrs. Hudson found a couple of chairs for them to sit in. J.L. reintroduced Maddie and J.L. to him.

J.L. then said "I want to tell you about your father, I got to spend time with him, but what I have to tell you is very sad. Your father was killed in a placed called The Painted Hills and I was with him". Then J.L. went on to tell him the story about how had met Gideon and spending time with his brother and sisters and how they hired him to search for him.

Joseph said "You came all this way to find me?" J.L. said "It seemed important to do and the least I could do for your father. I went all the way to Hell's Canyon and found your partner and he told me that you were sick, maybe had consumption, and were coming here to Prairie City. But I'm a thinkin' that's not what you have."

Joseph then said "No, I don't. It's much worse than that, and I know I'm gonna die."

Maddie couldn't help herself and asked "What do you think you have contracted Mr. Thomas?"

Joseph answered "I don't think I can prove it, but I think old Just Pitts poisoned me. I'm not sure with what, but it's eatin' up my insides."

'Just Pitts?' thought Maddie. Again, Maddie couldn't help herself and asked "Why would he do such a thing, um this Mr. Pitts, is that his name?"

"Greed and he's got no scruples," Joseph answered.

J.L. said, "Sir, the authorities need to know about this." Mrs. Hudson interrupted with "I've already talked to our local Sheriff."

Joseph spoke again, "Never mind about that now, I need to let you know that I have quite a bit of silver ore with me over at the Assayer's Office. If Mrs. Hudson will help me, I'll write a note so you all can look after it."

Mrs. Hudson scurried out of the room and was back within a minute with paper and pen. Joseph then dictated to her and as best he could he managed to sign his signature. Mrs. Hudson sensed that it was time to end the visit as he was tiring, and she ushered J.L. and Maddie out of the room. She then said "Now J.L. you'll be staying with us tonight too, correct?"

"Yes Ma'am, if I could, sure would appreciate it, but now I think we'll go straight over to that Assayer's Office and see what we can learn."

They walked back into town, located the little office, went in and emerged a half hour later with surprised looks on their faces. After a minute J.L. said, "Well that's quite a haul". And Maddie added "And that works out to quite a bit of money." 10% was to go to Mrs. Hudson, 80% to Joseph's family, and for their trouble, 10% to J.L. and Maddie!

With that out of the way but certainly not out of mind, J.L.'s stomach reminded him that he was hungrier than a bear again, "Can we get something to eat?" he asked. Maddie answered "Sure, I know just the place, but after that Mr., if you're thinking you're going to spend the night with me instead of your horse, you need to find the bath house!"

J.L. felt a little embarrassed thinking that the last time he'd had a good wash up was days ago in the Snake River. He said, a little plaintively "If I weren't so danged hungry I'd take that bath now, huh, or we can sit at separate tables."

"No, we'll just ask for one big table" Maddie laughed. J.L. chuckled too; and realized it had been some while since he had done that, and it felt good.

After their supper J.L. found the bath house. And as the day was drawing to a close he met Maddie back at the boarding house. It was a warm evening, but there was a breeze stirring. J.L. and Maddie found rocking chairs on a back porch, enjoying the evening and each other and catching up on the news both had to share. By the time that it began to get dark both were tired and they headed off to bed. Once tucked in J.L. couldn't decide what felt better, the bed or Maddie next to him. Then he decided that beds were a dime a dozen but there was only one Maddie. And in that quiet moment he remembered all the Lord had been doing in his life, and he felt most thankful.

Before they fell asleep, Maddie said a prayer for Joseph. "Lord, we don't understand all that is taking place. We don't understand the evil in some folks, like Pitts, but Lord, all we can pray for is Your will be done," she concluded.

Chapter Seven
The Little Ones

*"Whoever shall receive one of such children
in my name, receiveth me . . ."*
Mark 9:37

In the morning J.L. and Maddie discover that Joseph has died. Mrs. Hudson asks the two to sit in the parlor. Mrs. Hudson, being a Christian woman, guided him in making his peace with the Lord.

"He went peacefully and he knew where he was going. I believe there was a bit of a smile on his face at his last breath."

"Praise God for that" Said Maddie.

"What do you think would be best regarding his remains?" asks Mrs. Hudson of them.

J.L. answered that one, "I think the family would be fine to know he received a proper burial here. I will let them know and about your sacrificial care for him."

After breakfast with Mrs. Hudson, J.L. and Maddie returned to the Assayer's Office. They complete their transactions with the bank and brought Mrs. Hudson her portion in which she was overwhelmed with. They let Mrs. Hudson know that they were going to head for home. They also decided that Maddie was going to need a horse. And she was excited about that possibility; never enough horse flesh was her motto. At the livery stable where Gus has been boarded the man arranged for one. It was a sorrel mare, not too many hands, but what Maddie figured might be some good breed stock.

Goliath too, had been staying at the stable. The livery man had really taken to the big dog. But he upon seeing Maddie, he greeted her like a child might his long lost mother. It's just that his generous kisses were a whole lot wetter. There was a stop at the bank which arranged for a wire of the 80% of Joseph's earnings at the mine. Their share was stowed in the bottom of a saddle bag. By noon they were on their way heading west towards John Day, Mitchell, perhaps the Painted Hills if time allowed, and back home to The Dalles. It would take them the better part of the week.

It was quite a warm in the afternoon and J.L and Maddie stayed as close to the river and the shady elms and willows to keep man and beat cool. Goliath was convinced that a splash now and then was imperative.

J.L. enjoyed Maddie's company greatly and she caught him up on things at home while he shared the terrible adventure of Hell's Canyon.

She was shocked about the wolf attack, amused by the little girl that called J.L. a bear. She nearly spat when she heard about Clint Jeffers showing up. And she was absolutely shocked, yet mesmerized, by the account of the attack on the Chinese miners and Mai Lee. On the spot, as they rode, Maddie prayed for the Chinese miners, seeking God's protection and wisdom for them.

They continued to travel west until late in the day but there was still enough sun for J.L. try his luck for some trout. He hooked into a couple of fat trout and Maddie went about getting them fried for their dinner along with some potatoes and some greens she found up from the river.

The next day they traveled through John Day and Dayville. The third night they stayed just past a steep canyon and away from where the John Day River headed north. They no longer would have the river but there were small creeks that still flowed some even in the middle of summer.

That morning John and Maddie awoke with a start, both had been sleeping very soundly because the trip was beginning to take its toll. At first J.L. just wanted to shout at Goliath to be quiet, but he thought he could smell smoke. It wasn't their campfire because they had decided the night before not to have a campfire.

Maddie said "Do you smell smoke?" as she started to get up. J.L. remembered that they had no fire and so he was up on his feet too. Just to the west to them and over a little hill a dark plume of smoke rose. Goliath continued to bark wildly and Maddie thought she could hear the voices of people shouting or screaming. There was a little wind coming from the west which must have carried the sounds. J.L. was in his boots in a second and grabbed up his rifle, whispering to Maddie "We gotta' get that dog to shut up!" Maddie went over to Goliath and clamped her slim hand around his muzzle and whispered, "Shh, Shh, Shh" in his ear.

J.L. took off on a run to the top of the knoll. As he got to the top he crouched down then hit the ground laying flat looking over the edge for what he could see. Amongst the junipers by a little creek he noticed a covered wagon ablaze. He could hear the sound of whooping natives, as their voices were growing distant. He was quickly on his feet once again running down the hill and as he ran his first thought was 'this wagon seems familiar'. Within a moment, as he was entering the campsite, he noticed two bodies on the ground in front of him, a man and a woman. It was obvious they had been ravaged and murdered.

He set out next to work on putting the fire out right away. He was able to knock off the canvas top with the butt of his rifle. He then grabbed the bucket of water hanging on the wagon, throwing it towards the front seat. He ran to the little creek to fill the bucket up again and by the time he got back Maddie and Goliath had arrived. The second bucket of water put out the small fire burning on the buckboard.

Maddie immediately went to the two people lying on the ground, "Oh John this is horrible!" she wailed. J.L. ran to her, cupping his hand over her mouth, gesturing "Quiet Maddie". He half dragged her to the little creek behind some willows, with Goliath following along. There he whispered, "The war party just left, but we need to stay quiet for a bit in case they decide to come back". Maddie had begun to cry softly. Goliath whimpered as well. J.L. felt greatly saddened, but perplexed as well. 'Why does this wagon seem familiar?' he again thought to himself.

Then, it came to him; this was the same wagon he had met at the summit of the Blue Mountains weeks ago. It was that nice couple, the doctor and his wife, but wait, him thinking in split seconds, 'Where are the little girls?' "Maddie, I know those folks, where are the little girls? The ones I mentioned to you."

They both threw caution to the wind and started back towards the wagon. It was Maddie who noticed that the woman laying on the ground, with arm and hand extended, her index finger was pointed toward the wagon. Maddie instinctively reached out to the hand and noticed a little slip of paper in her clenched fist. She pried it from the dead woman's hand and opened it. Scrawled were four words "Look under the seat". J.L. raced to the wagon, climbed aboard, and like an angry bear tore the seats out of his way. He could hardly believe his eyes, there were the two little girls. They looked like they were sleeping soundly, but he was afraid they may be dead.

"Maddie, come quick"! She was up and in the wagon in a split second grabbing up the first little girl in her arms. "John, she's breathing, she's just asleep". John gathered up the other girl and they both headed to the creek. With a handkerchief Maddie washed the little girl's faces. But the girls continued to sleep. While they began to check the two out, she notice another slip of paper sticking out of an apron pocket of the older girl. Pulling it out she said "John, look!" opening it she said "it's a letter". She started to read it out loud. The hand writing was that of a woman with neat penmanship, saying "To whom this may concern. If you have found this, then you have found us dead, but have found our daughters hopefully alive. They are sleeping soundly because my husband, Dr. Jenkins, has given them enough Laudlum to put them to sleep. They will awake in a few hours. We did not know what else to do. The natives that have been following us for the last day or two, we just feared the worse."

The letter went on to convey who they were, that the girls were named Rachel and Esther. Their birth dates were indicated and with Maddie doing math in her head to realize that the older girl, Rachel was four and Esther was two. Also there was information regarding where they were from and where they were heading. As well as the name of a close relative they should contact back east.

While the girls slept J.L. and Maddie set about the unnerving chore of burying the couple. J.L. found a couple of shovels in their wagon, they found a secluded sandy spot near the creek, and did their best to give this young couple a proper burial. Afterwards,

Maddie knelt down near the graves and began to softly sing an old hymn. J.L. guessed this was the best they could to do to say the right words.

The girls slept through the rest of the day and that night as well. Maddie, though was worried that perhaps they'd had too much of the Laudlum, and she continue to check to make sure they were breathing. But the girls just continued to sleep soundly and peacefully. For reasons only Goliath could know, as night fell, he placed his huge body next to these little girls. J.L. decided that he would try to sit up through the night; found a tree to lean back against, rifle in his lap.

He thought he'd managed to stay awake during the night. The last thing he'd remembered was watching the Big and Little Dipper move around the North Star. But, all of a sudden he woke with a start with the feeling of a little finger prodding him in the chest. He opened his eyes to see a smiling little girl saying repeatedly "Bear-man, you're the Bear-man!"

J.L. said a silent "Thank you Lord," looking towards the Heavens, then gathered the little girl in his arms growled gently and lightly grazed his unshaven face against her soft skin. She let out a giggle. Then J.L. could see that Maddie was holding the other smaller girl in her arms and softly talking to her. The little girl was wide awake now and asking for her mommy. Maddie was lost in what to say, but simply said "Your Mommy and Daddy have gone to heaven." And then Maddie said "And we need to take you with us."

The older girl seemed to sense that this was alright. The little one continued to cry softly, but clung to Maddie.

J.L. got the horses ready and helped Maddie get on her horse with the little girl in her arms. He then mounted Gus, reached down his large hand and scooped up the little girl onto the saddle with him. The ride into Mitchell was down the hill following the creek. They made straight for Mitchell without stopping. Upon entering the little town, J.L. first went to the place he was familiar with, Brawdie's Blacksmith Shop. Brawdie was in and there with his assistant, busy on the job. The clanging of iron and smell of smoke was in the air. They looked up as J.L.'s large shadow fell across them.

"Is that you J.L.?" Brawdie asked, "and what in tarnation are you doing here?"

J.L. answered "It seems like I only come here to give you bad news." He then, quickly as he could, told Brawdie about what had taken place with the young family. When J.L. finished, Brawdie said "We have a new Sheriff in town and we need to go see him right away." They left the blacksmith shop and proceeded a few doors down to the small building and went inside and met Sheriff Miller. Once again J.L. told the story. The Sheriff said "I believe I know exactly who is responsible for this. It's a small band of no-good renegades that have been troubling ranchers and travelers for some time." He went on. "But they've never gone so far as to murder somebody." He finished.

The Sheriff said he was going to form a posse immediately and "Get right on it."

J.L. and Brawdie headed back, walked past the blacksmith shop a couple more doors down, to a little café where Maddie and the girls were. Once inside the two noticed that the little girls were busy devouring big slabs of French toast.

Once breakfast was done, J.L. thought that he should go visit Pastor Scott and give him the bad news as well. He did not find him at the church, but at his home. His wife, Cora was out front working in her flower and vegetable garden, invited them in. The Pastor was at a small desk in the corner by a window, large Bible open, writing paper was strewn about, obviously working on next Sunday's sermon.

"J.L., so nice to see you!" boomed the pastor. "What brings you back to town, and look at this, is this Maddie that you mentioned? And these little girls, I don't remember you mentioning daughters." His comment caught the Matthews off guard, and himself to thinking he had made a mistake of some kind.

"Yessir, this is my wife Maddie. And these girls, Sir, are Rachel and Esther".

The pastor shook the little girl's hands and smiled at them.

Maddie said, "J.L. I think I will take the girls outside for a bit and show them the garden."

J.L. filled in the Pastor with the news. The pastor was aware of the family and had heard of them coming. They were excited that a doctor might be in the area.

"Oh this is so terrible, Lord have mercy!" he said, with obvious grief in his voice. He thought for a moment and then asked J.L., "What are your plans for the little girls?"

"Pastor, I don't rightly know, I guess that is one of the reasons I wanted to see you. What should we do?" J.L. shared the information about the family with the pastor.

"I think there is no doubt that if you and Maddie were to take them to The Dalles and care for them that would be the best thing. You may need to talk with some legal counsel but them losing you at this point, the only ones they know . . . and, huh, Maddie, she looks the type who would tend to these girls well . . . I just think that would be another loss that would be too hard."

"Well, Sir, you are right, Maddie would look after those girls as if they were her own."

"Perhaps," said the pastor thoughtfully and carefully, "that is what God's plan is. His word says He works all things out for the good."

"Wait a minute, Pastor; are you saying this was God's plan that these girls lose their Mama and Papa?" The pastor's statement had taken J.L. aback. "Because that is one I can't even understand."

"No, no, J.L. let me explain as best as I can." The pastor opened his bible to the following verse. "This is in the book of Romans, Chapter 8, verse 28, I will write it down for you because it is something to think about especially with all that has happened to you." "*And we know that all things work together for good for them that love God, to them who are the called according to his purpose.*" Bad things happen, you know that, happens pretty much every day.

"Yep, and at times I guess I have done some of those things." J.L. said, hanging his head a bit.

"Yessir, we all have. We live under a curse of sin and bad happens. And this curse of sin we live under will go on for some time until this period of time is over and Jesus returns. We come to know Jesus then we turn from our bad ways but, of course, many do not. So God has made this promise for those who believe and for the likes of those children. What bad that has happened, He finds way to make some good out of it. You think about the circumstances of all that took place with that family, those little girls, you finding them just at the right time and they knowing you . . . why, it is nothing short of a miracle!"

"Now, these little girls will have a chance at life. And then there is the blessing for Maddie and you. I don't recall, pardon me, but you do have other children right, J.l.?"

"One son, named Jacob. We had another boy but he died as a baby sometime back when we were coming to Oregon. I nearly lost Maddie too. We had hoped for some more children, but she just didn't seem to be able to have anymore."

"I can't speak for God, but maybe this is just a fine example of how He works things out for the good. These girls need a mother and a father and, for Maddie, she gets to fulfill that desire to be a mother at least for a while.

J.L. and Maddie stayed for the night with the pastor and his wife. They started out the next morning with their saddle bags full of what they would need to get home. There, however, only seemed two options of transport, one was a wagon or by horse. For expediency they decided they would go by horse.

Travel with the girls took a better part of the week with lots of rest stops along the way. There was no opportunity to see the Painted Hills the most direct route needing to be taken.

Chapter Eight
The Right Thing To Do

"In whom also we have obtained an inheritance, being predestined according to the purpose of him who worketh all things after the counsel of his own will."
Ephesians 1:11

The Matthews rode into their little ranch on a late, warm and breezy Friday afternoon. The girls were more than ready to get down from the horses and stretch legs that were ready to run and jump. J.L. and Maddie were just ready to stretch out in their beds and hope for a long night's sleep.

From the chicken coop, Jacob heard the commotion and dashed out to see to his surprise, mother, father and the two little girls. He didn't get a chance to ask many questions because Goliath thought a wet greeting was more important. In a flat second Jacob was on the ground with Goliath happily pouncing on him and licking his face.

When he had untangled himself from the big dog, Jacob took off across the yard to the waiting arms of his parents. Mrs. Valdez appeared from the door, apron around her portly waist. "Ah senor, senora, you are home! Oh, and who these little senoritas!" she said, coming down from the porch.

Rachel and Esther were now trying to hide a bit behind Maddie. "Come on girls, say hello", she said, guiding the little girls out from behind her. "This is my son, Jacob and that nice lady is Mrs. Valdez. They will be very glad to know you. These fine young ladies are Rachel and Esther."

Soon they were all ushered into the house. Mrs. Valdez seemed to create a huge dinner out of what would have been just for Jacob and her. Jacob was willing to give up his bed for the girls, the deal being him getting to spend the night out under the stars. J.L. escorted Mrs. Valdez home and returned just as it was getting dark. By the time he got home the little girls were asleep.

Jacob had already found a grassy spot near the porch to camp out. He was stretched out in a pile of straw and some old horse blankets.

J.L. said, "Mind if I join you for a bit?"

"No, Pa, you can stay the whole night ifin' you want," said Jacob.

"Thanks for the offer, Pard, but my bed, after a month out would be too hard to turn down. What'd you think about those little girls?"

"Well, they sure are cute and kind of silly but, uh, are they going to live with us forever?

"That I don't know, surely for the time being though until we can talk to their relatives back in Pennsylvania."

"I was always kinda hopin' for another brother..." Jacob started but didn't know what else to say.

"Yep, we too but it just wasn't to be. But sisters are good, I have two. And they are younger than me."

"And did you like them Pa?" Jacob's faced scrunched up like maybe he had just tasted lemon.

"Well, yeah, most of the time," J.L. laughed. "These little girls need us to be there Ma and Pa right now and having you to be there older brother and help them along would be really helpful."

"I'll give it a go."

"That would be the most we could ask."

~~~

Later that night, although not too much later, J.L and Maddie were in their own bed. She had her head on J.L.'s chest. J.L. was doing all he could to keep his eyes open but Maddie was chattering away.

Maddie was beginning to wind down; she had discussed the whole of the adventure. "What do you think God thinks of all this and what does He wants us to do?"

"Maddie, I am sure am not one to speak for God but I guess He will let us know. He has been pretty good at doing so, so far. In the meantime, we just do what we are supposed to do, as the Good book would say."

"You are right, and that is just exactly what we will do. Read the bible more and try to do what it says in light of all these circumstances."

~~~

The next day was Saturday, and J.L. was tired as was Maddie but there was a lot of catch up that seemed to need to be done. Jacob and the neighbor boys had done a good job of keeping up on the chores. Their house was spotless as Mrs. Valdez had left it. J.L. wondered about sleeping arrangements for the girls. He expected for the time being Jacob was happy to camp outside. But, now there was about a month left of summer. Maddie planned on going to the telegraph office on Monday and sending a short message to the children's only living great aunt. Evidently there were no grandparents living or brothers and sisters of their parents. She would write a longer letter explaining all the details.

On Sunday, the five went to church and this drew much interest as the little girls came along too. In fact, the pastor pulled the Matthews aside after the service to find out more about this.

On Monday, before the Matthews had really even started the day, the pastor and a crew of ten or so men showed up with tools and a wagon load of lumber. Before the day was out, there was a new room added on to the house – the girls' new bedroom!

At the end of that wonderful day, as Maddie set out to feed the volunteers out on some makeshift tables under the trees a few women from the church showed up with baskets full of food as well. This turned into quite a banquet. A breeze had come up to take the sting out of the hot day. As they all gathered Maddie spoke up. "I just cannot thank you all enough. To think just this weekend we were thinking that we would need to get busy and improve our accommodations and now here we our . . ." Her voice trailed off and some emotion filled her throat.

The pastor jumped right in, "J.L. and Maddie, this is truly what the bible says, "It is more blessed to give than to receive. We are the blessed ones." There were murmurs among the men and woman that indicated their agreement. "And if I may, Matthews' family, may I offer a prayer to our good Lord who has provided us with much." J.L. and Maddie nodded. All bowed their heads.

"Lord, we thank Thee so much for Thy great mercy. We thank Thee for J.L., Maddie and Jacob and their desire to give these little girls a home. We are grateful to Thee for giving us opportunities to share your love with others. May you rich bless their lives and including these little ladies, Rachel and Esther. We know the enemy meant to harm them but you, Oh Lord, watched over them. It is truly nothing short of a miracle what Thou hast done. We ask, Lord, for blessing upon this family and this home. May they prosper in You as they seek to do Your will in all things. We also thank Thee for Your provision, which, by the way, smells so good. So Lord, be at our table, please and in Your Name Amen."

The next day Maddie rode into town by herself to go to the telegraph station and stop at the General Store for some much needed items for the girls.

At the telegraph office she told the clerk what she needed to send. "But, frankly, how do you say that in just a few words?"

"That is a tough one, Ma-am. I see it now and then and other than to just be forthright, I don't know what else to tell you."

Maddie sent the following message. 'Your grand nieces, Rachel and Esther are with us. They are fine. Seth and Molly have died, killed by renegades. Please advise us about the girls. I will send a letter. Very sorry."

Two days later the Western Union messenger brought a message to Maddie from the great aunt. It said. "Very sad, I am heartbroken. I am unable to travel such a distance. I will respond to your letter. Blessings to you for taking care of the girls."

Maddie wrote a detailed letter about all that had taken place, leaving out some more of the grizzly details. She assured the Aunt about who they were and that they were Christian folk and people who were most able and glad to take care of the girls.

A couple of weeks later a letter came from Pennsylvania from the great aunt. In short she explained that she was an invalid and not really able to travel or for that matter take care of the girls. She thought that she could find a good home for them back in Pennsylvania with friends. She would pay for their return trip. She also indicated that perhaps it would be best for the girls to remain with the Matthews. Upon reading that portion Maddie's heart leaped in her throat. She felt both glad and guilty at the same time. J.L. was in town that day at the Blacksmiths shop so she would have to wait until he got home that evening to tell him the surprising news. She was not sure she could wait so long.

~~~

During this same time there was another meeting of two men, Jeffers and the little old man. The meeting was once again held in the well appointed study of the latter's. It was again at night, as if that was a cloak of secrecy in its self. Once again there was an open whiskey bottle and glasses. Jeffers had already helped himself twice to the amber liquid.

The little man was again quite irritated. "I have had just about enough of your clumsiness on this Jeffers. Once again the job was not done. Matthews is back in town, alive as you and me. I am not paying you another red cent until this done." The little man's voice was rising in tone and emotion. "How hard can this be, I shoulda done it myself."

This time though, Jeffers was not being bluffed by this fellow. "Well, you know what, you little skinflint, that is just what you can do. Do it yourself. I have had enough a belly full of this business." Jeffers was now on his feet, he was fueled by the whiskey and he was mad, face as red as his old logger's coat.

"That is not our deal!" shouted the man as he rose to his feet in indignation as well.

At that Jeffers reached across the desk and with clenched fist, hit the man smack in the face. He collapsed into his chair but hit it at angle this, in turn, propelled him out of the chair and to the floor. Jeffers was around the desk and over him in a heartbeat. This time he had a knife in his hand, the point of it heavily resting on the man's Adam Apple. "You got a couple of choices here, struggle and die where you lay or lie still. The man chose the latter. Jeffers then stood up but placed a heavy boot on the man's throat where the knife had been. He reached down and pulled the wallet out of the man's coat and stuffed it in his.

"What is ever in here will be payment enough I think for all my trouble. I don't imagine you will be going to the sheriff, hard to explain but just in case you think you might here is this." And with that Jeffers punched the man in the face and then kicked him in the gut, knocking the wind from him.

It wasn't his plan to kill the man but to disable him long enough to get on his way. Has Jeffers rode off he spit and vowed on that to never return to this part of Oregon again. There were other fish to fry maybe down in Nevada or California and he aimed to find out.

~~~

That last month of summer seemed to go so fast with all that needed to be done. J.L. had planned on going to Goldendale sooner rather than later but it wasn't until mid-September that he had a chance. Swen the Blacksmith had ended up with some big jobs and enlisted J.L.'s help.

In the first part of that month Maddie had a strange occurrence that made her wonder. She had made some cookies with the girls help, which meant the process took twice as long but she figured with all those little hands helping those cookies would be twice as sweet.

She decided to take some to Mr. Larsen across the way and introduce the girls to him proper. As they stepped off of their property, started across the road she could see that he was talking with a man in a surrey. She didn't want to bother so started to turn back when she saw that the surrey was leaving. As the surrey swept by her she saw little of the man who wasn't looking her way. But, yet, he seemed familiar, she just couldn't quite put it together why.

As she and the girls got to Mr. Larson's front porch, she shouted out. "Morning Mr. Larson, I have brought a surprise for you and want you to meet some very special ladies."

"Well, lookee there! What pretty girls and it looks like you brought something for my sweet tooth also. Can you come and sit a spell, Maddie?"

"Certainly, but just for minute, I seem to have my hands pretty full these days."

Once settled she gave the girls a cookie each and shooed them to play under a big willow. Mr. Larson had gone in for coffee and the two of them settled back in old rockers.

"Those little fair ones a visiting for a spell?" he asked when they were settled with cookies and coffee. Maddie could hardly wait to tell him the story.

"Well, isn't that just something? I am so glad you told me. You know if I can help in anyway . . ."

"I almost didn't come over; I noticed you had company, the man in the surrey."

"Oh, him," Mr. Larson's voice dropped. Maddie gave him a curious look.

"No, no, that was just my brother."

"I didn't know you had a brother here" said Maddie.

He's from over in Rowena, owns that big house on the cliff. Maybe you've seen it. Anyway, we just don't see eye to eye. In fact I can't remember the last time we talked.

"Is everything alright?" Maddie's curiosity was getting the better of her. And there was that sense that somehow he was familiar. She just got a glance and maybe it was that he looked a bit like Mr. Larsen and then she remembered that his face and nose seemed to have a bandage on it.

"Fine with me but, not so fine for him. He rode all the way over here for some liniment our mother use to make. I always keep some on hand I am always getting banged up by something. He came for that. I patched him up a bit. It looks like he got his nose broken. Says he fell down but . . ."

Again Maddie's look was more like a question. "Well, after all these years you just recognize things and to me it looks like someone punched him good. But then he ain't exactly the type for a fist fight. He is a little more underhanded that. Anyway, enough about him. Tell me more about your plans for those little girls." It was obvious that he wanted to change the subject.

Maddie wanted to ask him, somehow, how he might have looked familiar to her but she would have to wait.

~~~

One morning Friday in mid September, J.L. told Maddie, "I need to go see the Thomas'. I had planned to do it sooner."

"There is no reason you couldn't go tomorrow," said Maddie. "Maybe, you could even take Jacob, give him a little break from the girls," Maddie added with a little laugh.

"I think that is a very good idea. We'd try to just be gone for the day, if we leave early enough. I just feel like I need to see them in person and just share more with them. I know we wired them and you sent a little letter but I think a meeting would be good."

The next morning J.L. and Jacob left early. Goliath stayed behind, he had become the little girl's constant companion although they subjected him to all kinds of girlish play. He didn't even seem to mind wearing a bonnet now and then.

J.L. and Jacob enjoyed the time together. For Jacob this was nothing short of grand adventure. He was very excited about the ferry crossing. J.L. chit-chatted with the ferry captain telling him of his adventure and about Joseph.

The two Matthews men, when on top of the hills took a few minutes to take in the view. From where they were they could see Mt. Hood, Mt. Adams, which seemed huge against the sky and off to the distance Mt. St. Helens and off to the distance, Mt. Rainer, which looked much smaller that the Behemoth of a mountain it was. The sky was as blue as blue could be while the fields of grain had begun to turn to amber waiting for harvest.

After going to Abigail's store J.L. once again met the Thomas family at the ranch just north of town.

"J.L. we appreciate you so much making that trip for us," said Benjamin. He was getting around pretty good from his injured knee but still using a cane.

"And for you to find Joseph and the way that it all happened, well, I think it is nothing short of a miracle."

J.L. responded, "My wife says there were a few miracles that took place." He then went on to tell them about the little girls that they now had with them at home.

"Glory be!! But oh, such evil too," exclaimed Hannah.

"We have put all the money that Joseph willed to the family and designated strictly for ministries, and specifically for the circuit riders."

That reminded J.L. that he had an opportunity or two to talk with people who knew of Gideon but his plan to share more with other people on the return trip was obviously changed.

Abigail approached the subject. "J.L. have you thought about what God wants you to do from here? Certainly you will have your hands full with caring for those girls now."

"Ma'am, you are right, that seems to be the most important thing at the moment. I don't really see myself as a circuit rider, umm, I wouldn't even know where to start such a thing. Uh, don't get me wrong, that would be a most honored profession. It certainly is something to strike out across the country here abouts and I have always had a bit of wanderlust – you know, what's over the next hill. But now that the Good Lord has seen fit to give my family back and now these additions."

"One thing, I hope you have noticed, J.L., if it wasn't for you think what would have happened to some innocent people, the Chinese girl and those little bundles now at home. I hope you can see now how God has really used you."

"Frankly, I haven't thought about it. I sure wouldn't want to take any credit. I guess the most I can say for that is the Lord put me in the right place at the right time but . . ."

"It should be gratifying for you because you were pretty hard on yourself the last we met."

"What we want you to know, is that if you feel this call, we will support you, get you some training, whatever you would need."

"Well, thanks but, I will have to give that a great deal of thought. I will let Maddie know and I know she will make it a matter of prayer. And as far as traipsing off, well, that would be interesting, as long as it isn't that ole Hells Canyon – I am in no hurry to return there, if ever."

Not surprising, J.L. and Jacob started later than they had planned. They got to the ferry making its last trip for the day. The sun now set low as twilight began. J.L. decided that they would just camp by the river for the night. He was not concerned that Maddie would be worried, if they didn't show up by night, she knew they would be staying out that night.

They had brought provisions for the night; it was simple but ample enough to get them through until the next day. They wandered up and down the river banks, skipping stones and picking up objects that interested them. Jacob found what they thought was an old fishhook carved from bone a long time ago by a native.

They camped just a few feet up from the river on the sandy beach. The wind had picked up and the breeze was from the east and cool so a warming fire was in order. The two of them lay down early as soon as the stars appeared. They talked about many things during the evening. J.L. was trying to remember if he had so many questions for his Pa when he was that age. He imaged so. Jacob didn't necessarily convey it but he relished this time alone with his father. But it seemed as if it was in mid-sentence when he fell asleep.

J.L. lingered a little longer. He was praying for more what he thought was just a conversation with the invisible but very present feeling God of the entire universe. It was questions too, rambling thoughts as well as he pondered to God about just what he was now to be doing.

But when he did drop off to sleep it seemed as if he had only been asleep but a moment. When he opened his eyes the sun was up, shining brightly on the river. Jacob still slept next to him. But there was a noise that he couldn't quite distinguish among the sounds of water, breeze and birds and such. It was the sound of moaning. He leaned a little closer to Jacob to see if he was making the noise in his sleep but it was not him. The horses were some feet off, hobbled but in the midst of tall grass, making the best of breakfast.

No, this was something else. He sat up, looked around his surrounding and noticed what, at first, he thought was a piece of large of drift wood that had come to shore just down from where they slept. As best as he could tell this is where the sound was emitting. As he rubbed the sleep out of his eyes and peered closer. It looked like maybe the log had some cloth tangled on it. This did not seem right and in a flash he was up moving quickly towards the log. The moaning was louder and that is when he noticed that this was a person, a man looking mostly drowned.

But it wasn't just a man it was one that J.L. knew — none other than the Chinese miner Chang. Not only did he look mostly drowned but it was obvious he had been injured or physically assaulted.

"Chang, Chang, can you hear me?" J.L. spoke loudly to him and at the same time trying to gently drag him from the river towards the fire.

Chang opened his eyes, blinking and trying to focus. "You, J.L. San, is it you?" he said weakly.

"Yep it is me and I am going to help you." J.L. said trying to be comforting in his word. By this time Jacob had woken and was up. "Pa?" he started to ask.

But J.L. interrupted by saying, "Son, find some wood and see if you can kick up that fire. This man needs warming and our blankets."

Soon they had him bundled in their two blankets and close to the fire. J.L attempted to wash the sand and some blood from Chang's face. Chang was trying to talk but J.L. told him to save his breath for a bit. He got coffee going and after a bit gave some to Chang. "This isn't that fixing tea you gave me but it should help warm you a bit." He said holding the cup to Chang's lips. Chang took sips and sighed a bit as if it must have tasted or felt good.

Chang laid there for some time. His color returned and so J.L. asked him if he wanted to try some food. During that short convalescence J.L. briefed to Jacob that, yes, he did know this man. "Remember me telling you about the Chinese miners, this is one of them, this is my friend Chang."

J.L. sopped some bread in the coffee and Chang hungrily ate it. There wasn't much but it seemed to revive him. J.L. asked, "Chang do you feel like you have some bones broken?"

"No, I not think so" said Chang, he was trying to rise to a sitting position and with some help did.

"What are you doing here, in the river, where are the others . . . where is May Lee?"

Chang in brief words told them that his partners had been gunned downed and that May Lee has been carried off.

"Did you see who did this?" asked J.L.

"No, at night" Change paused, then added, "but I think it just one person. He comes in shooting, bullet hit me, I lay still like dead. May Lee not shot but she is carried off."

"Where were you hit?"

Chang turned his head, and at the side, J.L. could see a crease, a bloody line about two inches that was mostly scabbed up.

"Why are you here in the river?" J.L. asked.

"I come to find you. You, please, J.L. San, go find and get Mai Lee!"

For a second J.L. wasn't sure that he heard Chang correctly. But the look on Chang's face told him that is exactly what he heard. And certainly he would be the most likely candidate to that and as he realized the ramifications of such a trek, J.L. felt his heart sink in his chest.

Chapter Nine
The Reckoning

"Violence shall no more be heard in thy land, wasting nor destruction within thy borders; but thou shalt call thy walls Salvation, and thy gates Praise."
Isaiah 60:18

J.L. knew that he needed to get Jacob and himself home by nightfall yet he wanted to see if he could let Chang rest. And then there was the-how-do-we-get-him-home question. He decided to see the ferryman and see if he had a way to get a wagon that he could carry Chang home in. He decided to leave Jacob and ride the little bit back to the ferry and see if they thought they might help.

Sara was there, the ferryman's daughter. He told her of his plight.

"Mr. Matthews, we have one right here, back behind the shed. Ain't pretty but it will probably do what you need. Pa will be right along; he is on his way back with passengers."

It was fine with the ferryman; he even supplied two horses as well. Soon J.L. had the wagon hitched and was back to Jacob and Chang. They lifted Chang as gently into the wagon as possible trying to provide enough cushion for him with their bedrolls and long dried grass Jacob pulled. He let Jacob continue on his horse and J.L. drove the wagon. --- accompanied them, she would drive the wagon back. The trip seemed to take forever with the slow speed they went. Sara talked a mile a minute about everything under the sun. J.L. guessed maybe she didn't get a chance to use up all the words the Good Lord seemed to allot the womenfolk every day.

By sunset they were rolling into the property. Maddie was out front with the two girls. All of them cuddled into a rocking chair while she read them a picture book.

"John, is that you – and the wagon and who is this young lady, and oh my, who is that in the wagon? Is he alive John?" she said and to herself at the same moment thought, 'he sure has been full of surprises since he straightened out.'

"Mr. Chang are you alright?' J.L. said while jumping from the wagon. "Maddie this is Sara, she is the ferryman's daughter. I think I told you about her. In the wagon is Mr. Chang."

And with that of hearing his name Chang sat up and looked around.

"Mr. Chang?! You mean from Hells Canyon, Mr. Chang?" She was about to ask what and why but decided to not when seeing that the Chinese man looked worse for wear.

"Here Maddie help me get him out and into a bed" said J.L., thus bringing Maddie back to matters at hand.

Maddie decided it would be their bed; they would make do in the barn. Sleeping arrangements were sparse for more than just this new extended family.

Once tucked in, Maddie got busy in the kitchen making a broth for Chang. J.L. would have liked to have fetched the doctor but it was now already after dark. Jacob and the little girls were as curious as could be and kept trying to peek in the door but Maddie shooshed them out. Chang was conscious and was grateful for the soup. He ate what he could but was soon asleep.

The parents, now of three, got everyone settled down for the night, which was not so easy with this activity going on. They finally settled down in the main room.

Maddie started, "John, did he come looking for you?"

"Yes he did. You remember me telling you about Mai Lee. She really is no more than a girl, probably not quite out of her teen years. She has been taken and Chang's partners have been killed. He managed to escape and somehow managed to float the river, well I don't know, anyway, to get to me, thinking I could help."

"Help how?" Maddie said. "Can you go to the authorities, can they contact authorities back there, can someone go looking . . ." Maddie's voice trailed off. She could tell by the look on J.L.'s face that the likelihood of anything like that happening far enough down the line to find the girl probably would not happen.

"This sounds terrible and I'd like to think it not so true, but one Chinese girl probably would be low on the list" said J.L. matter of fact.

Maddie was quiet for a moment but it didn't take her long to realize what was being now considered. "He wants you to go get her doesn't he John?" she said soberly and in a near hush.

J.L. just nodded.

"Oh, Lord in heaven, no!" said Maddie in what could only be described as a quiet wail. Tears were in her eyes and her hand was covering her mouth.

J.L. reached his arms around her, pulled her to his chest and just held her for the longest time. He did it not just for her but himself as well.

After some time and with little being said by both of them, they made do in a pile of hay and blankets in the barn to attempt some sleep. For J.L., much to his surprise, he slept like a log until first light. Maddie was up and down checking on her charges and trying not to fret herself into a state with the reality J.L. would leave again and perhaps on a much more dangerous mission. She would not let him go alone; somehow the authorities would have to help. She would send him off to fetch the doctor but also to see Marshal James.

J.L. was up with a start. Only Maddie was up, everyone still slept.

"Maddie, did you sleep, how is Chang?"

"Yes, I did a bit. He seemed to sleep most of the night. I got him some water and a cool cloth for his head. That seemed to help. But we need to get the doctor right away. And, John, please, on this one go talk with Marshal James about this. I guess I know you have to go but you cannot do this on your own . . . you just can't!"

"I will do as you say."

Maddie handed him a cup of coffee and a biscuit. "I will have a real breakfast for you when you get back but doctor first and then, before you come home, the Marshal's office."

J.L. headed straight to town but with a quick stop at Mrs. Valdez to enlist her help. He hooked up her little wagon and she was soon on her way. He was able to find the doctor just getting in, explained and this kind soul who just seemed to work the most endless hours, was soon on his way.

Next it was the Marshall's office. The Marshall was in as well as Caleb too. J.L. quickly, but with detail, told them the story. He finished up with, "Sir, what can be done?"

"That is a good question, J.L. I don't think I have an easy answer to that one. But you going on your own, that is a very bad idea."

The look on J.L.'s face came across as a question as in 'then what?'

"Give me a few hours to think this over. I will see what we might be able to do. I will send a telegram to my superior and we will just see. I will come by later."

J.L. turned tail and headed back home. When he arrived, Dr. Brown was in their bedroom looking in on Chang. Mrs. Valdez was there making herself busy helping Maddie make breakfast. Jacob was out in the chicken coop with the girls gathering eggs.

"How did it go with the Marshall?" was the first sentence out of Maddie's mouth.

"I don't know, he didn't have an answer right away. Said he needed to send a telegram and he would come by later. How about with the Doc?"

"I don't know either yet."

Mrs. Valdez was out gathering the children and Maddie was getting the table set when the Doctor came out of the room.

"Well, folks, Mr. Chang has certainly been through a trial. I think it would have killed most. I can't imagine what must all have happened. But, the good news is I think he will be fine. No broken bones as I can tell, just lots of bruises and bumps. A week or two of rest and food should help him recover. Best not to move him for a day or so just so we can keep the pain at bay."

After breakfast, Mrs. Valdez, as she was getting ready to leave said, "You give me Mr. Chang, uh, I mean, I take care of him like I did Senor J.L. You bring him in the wagon, two days from now. Yes, that is what we do." She said the last little sentence like it was a command not a consideration.

Later that day, in the early afternoon Marshal James rode in with Caleb. J.L. was out in the barn and Maddie in the house. She invited them but they declined choosing rather to sit on the front porch. They were glad to have coffee and some cookies Maddie provided.

"J.L." started the Marshal. "I wired my boss, I, uh, pulled some strings, I guess and this is what we came up with – ain't much. I can proceed to help you it's just resources but other law enforcement over that way are pretty slim to none for something extra like this. Gear and horses and such we can provide in Baker City. I talked with Caleb about this, though, and we can send him with you. He is willing to go. But it would be just you and him. And about two weeks away is about what could be afforded. We would need to put on someone else while he is gone. I don't know if that is reasonable; there, hopefully find the girl and back." This thought stopped the marshal; he took off his hat, scratched his head and asked for some more coffee.

"But you are willing to go, Caleb?" asked Maddie.

"Yes, Ma-am, I am," was all of Caleb's response.

J.L. thought for a moment, took another sip of his coffee and said, "I don't think I could ask for anything more."

"Is the time frame reasonable?" said the marshal but shrugging his shoulders.

"Don't know." Then J.L. added, "but I think I know where to look for her – could be wrong though."

"You think you have an idea of who might have her?" jumped in Maddie.

"I do, can't really tell you why, just something nagging at my noggin."

"When would you want to leave, J.L.?" asked Caleb.

J.L. was quiet for a minute, in fact everyone was. He didn't want to look at Maddie, chose to stare at the ground then said. "First light."

"I will be ready then", said Caleb. "I will take care of supplies this afternoon and if you meet me first thing at the office then we will be off."

"There is one other thing, J.L." the marshal started, "I will need to deputize you as deputy marshal. Just as a volunteer, no pay involved."

The look on J.L.'s face was that of "I guess it is possible that pigs can fly too."

~ ~ ~

Caleb and J.L. met up bright and early, just before the sun. Besides his horse Caleb had another. J.L. too, besides saddling Gus had another sturdy horse out with bridle on. It was a fairly new one that Maddie had acquired.

The thought was they could do more miles by trading horse every few hours and get along farther in the course of day. The plan was to ride until after twilight each day until they made their destination. Even still it would take days, J.L. estimated a full week.

At that hour Jacob was up, Maddie was busy, the little girls slept as well as Chang. And as hard as it was to for Maddie to say goodbye she did so without great ceremony but holding J.L. tight and whispering in his ear a prayer and "I love you more than life it's self. Do what needs to be done but please be careful."

They rode hard that day with a longer break early afternoon for food, water and stretch. They camped that first night near the river. A fire was needed. Maddie, and evidently someone for Caleb, had packed them well for the next few days. However they would need to buy provisions in LaGrande or Baker City.

A few more days of this went by, along the Columbia River, then departing from that over the hills and through the many valleys that made up the area. Then it was across the Blue Mountains and by mid-afternoon on the fifth day they rode into Baker City. Here they boarded the horses found a café that served generous portions and checked into a hotel. They both slept long and hard. The next day after a more leisurely breakfast, they got more supplies and then headed out for

Hells Canyon. Three days later they rode into Oxbow heading for Andy's ranch. It was still warm and had a late summer feel to the area. Caleb had never been to this area and marveled at the grand expanse of river and cliffs.

They rode into Andy's place. He was obviously most surprised to see J.L. He invited them both in eagerly wanting to know why in the world they were back.

Over dinner that night J.L. told all that had happened.

"I will go with you. I know the canyon better than you, maybe I will be a help in finding that girl." Andy said.

"We would appreciate the help. But I have an idea of where she might be" Said J.L.

"You do?" both Andy and Caleb asked. J.L. had not shared his thoughts with Caleb wanting to ponder them on the way.

"I think the same hombre' that did Joseph in, his partner."

"Why do you think that?" said Caleb.

"For days I could not tell you why, just something scratching at the back of my head. Like some bit of a memory. Something I remember him saying in passing," said J.L.

"Did he know of the Chinese miners do you think?" asked Andy.

"I am sure, not that he said anything. I am sure, right as rain, that he is loony and in a dangerous way. I think he would be capable of most anything. How do you just go and poison your partner?" J.L. said.

Before first light the next morning J.L., Caleb and Andy headed out. This time they brought just one horse with them, with the hope that it would be for Mai Lee's to ride out. On the second day they got within range of the mine. They picked a place that gave them sighting distance up the canyon and behind some rocks. Here they would just watch. Caleb had brought a spy glass and could make out whatever activity might take place. They would camp here, but that meant no fire for that night.

"So what do we do?" asked J.L.

"I think we just watch for a while," said Caleb. "I actually have two arrest warrants on this fella, although one of them would be hard to stick – and that is regarding Joseph. I am not sure that it could ever be proven that he was poisoned. But it might be our way to come a knockin' if we don't see Mai Lee."

"Could you actually bring him in based upon that?" J.L. asked.

"Yep, may not stick. A judge would have to consider it but it would get him into custody for a time. But if we can just hang off for a while, maybe Mai Lee will appear. Or we can sweep the place carefully with the spy glass and see if there is anything that would imply that she was there."

The day was growing long and there seemed to be little that was going on. But after a while Just Pitts was spotted coming out of the mine. He was alone. He proceeded to the cabin and there he stayed all night. Although they could make out two sides of the hut two sides were not visible. Which one of the hidden sides the door was on they did not know.

A dim lantern light burned in the night for a short while but by 10PM it was out and there was no movement until the morning. At around 8AM again Pitts emerged from the cabin and proceeded back to the mine. No one else seemed to be seen.

The three of them watched for a couple of hours but no one showed. J.L. was becoming very impatient.

"Caleb, let me go down there. If he sees me, maybe he won't think me a threat because he has seen me before. I will cross the river here; on foot and go by the part of the cabin we can't see."

"I don't know," said Caleb doubt in his voice.

"I'll even go unarmed if that would help" J.L. added.

"No, I don't think that is a good idea but all you have is your rifle. Here take this pistol, tuck it in your belt and keep it out of sight just in case. Meanwhile Andy and I will keep our aim up if he should appear. You keep alookin' back now and then, we will wave if you need to make yourself scarce."

J.L. could wade the river but for one section. This he had to swim awkwardly for some feet with the gun held high in one hand. Once on the other bank though, he dipped in behind some tall willows. He could stay fairly hidden in them until he was just a few feet from the cabin. Once near the cabin, he approached it on the East side. Sure enough there was a little door in the back. As he got near the door, just a few feet away, he tripped over something that sent him to the ground. He quickly got to his feet at a crouch but did not take time to look at what it was. Arriving at the door, he noticed it slightly a jar. As he pushed it he could see a small form sitting on the floor. It was shadowy and he could not make out if it were Mai Lee.

His thought was, though, 'who else?' So he started to speak up in a low whisper when all of a sudden he heard the sound of a rifle being discharged and at the same time a bullet slammed near him in the door frame showering splinters. He dove in the door as another shot was fired, this one hit him in the boot and he felt the pain of something grazing his heal. He could also feel the warmth of blood in his boot and he knew he had been hit. Now he crawled inside and kicked the door closed.

The person in the dark corner let out a little shriek. It was certainly a feminine voice and J.L. was all but convinced now, that indeed it was Mai Lee. Another shot was fired, this one hitting the door, but by now J.L. was across the room next to the person.

"Mai Lee is that you?"

"Oh, is that you J.L. San?" she shrieked.

"Yes." He was now all but on her covering her with his body.

"He has a trap, you tripped over wire. It rings bell up in the mine that is how he must know you are here."

He expected to hear another shot but didn't. He guessed Pitts wasn't going to waste any more bullets plus accidently shoot his captive. J.L. looked Mai Lee and could see that she was bound at the wrists with a long leather strap. A pulled a pocket knife from his pocket and cut her loose. He wondered what the chances would be if they tried to make their escape out the front door. Were Caleb and Andy closer and ready to fire off if they tried to make their escape? It was not a question he wanted to bank on. But what was the chance of Pitts coming though the door firing? He didn't think that would be the case either so for the moment they would just sit tight.

J.L. asked, "Mai Lee are you alright, has he hurt you in anyway?"

"No, I am alright. He hit me sometimes when I try to escape but I am good now."

"Chang find you and is he alright too?" she asked.

"Yep, he is fine."

J.L was wracking his brain on what he could do next. There was the window at the front, a cloth hanging over. He shimmied over to it, but his foot was giving him some pain. He reached up to move the cloth to look out but the greasy oilskin was too hard to see out of. He took the same knife and slashed the thin material and peeked though without raising his head too much in view if the shooter was watching the window. He could see the river, upstream a bit to the rocks where Caleb and Andy were but they were not in sight.

Everything was eerily quiet and the moments seemed to go on forever. J.L. turned to look back at Mai Lee when he saw movement right in front of him. Caleb's head popped into view in front of the window.

"Shhh", whispered Caleb. "Is Mai Lee in there? Is she alright?"

"Yep, he had her tied up in her but she is fine."

"We heard gun shots?"

"Nicked me in my foot, but I'm alright. He is up in the mine, knew I was down here 'cause I tripped a wire, rang a bell up there." J.L. tried to explain using a few words.

"Alright, you stay there. Andy is behind a rock but has a good view of the mine. I am going up there, call for him to surrender but if he tries to shoot first Andy will take him down." And with that Caleb disappeared from the window.

A few minutes passed and then J.L. could hear Caleb shout. "Mr. Justin Pitts I am here to arrest you. I'm arresting you for holding Mai Lee, I am also arresting you for the suspicion of murder of one Joseph Thomas! Don't make this hard on yourself. Throw out your weapons and come along peaceably!"

"I ain't comin' out! You got no call to be bothering me!" shouted Justin Pitts from a distance.

"You don't come out, we come in. I got a posse here and some sharpshooters so do yourself a favor and give it up now! I will promise you a fair trial." Then he added, "You've got one flat minute to decide." J.L. chuckled a little to himself on that one, thinking, "Yeah, we are quite a posse of sharp shooters. But what that old coot doesn't know, might save him and us all." But his other thought was, 'the guy is goosy as can be, this might spook him."

Everything got quiet again. And the seconds dragged like minutes. But then, all of a sudden, it was as if all calamity broke loose. First there was a muffled 'pop', then a few short seconds and larger explosions, then a rumbling that came from the mine all the way to the cabin. The shaking was something else and the cabin began to shake violently as if in an earthquake. Dust began to spew through any opening there was. J.L. leapt back to Mai Lee, covering with her body just as the whole place came down around and an on them.

The two just lay there for a minute waiting for the falling and dust to subside. Coughing ensued as they had to take a breath. J.L. got up first, then literally picked up Mai Lee to her feet.

"Are you hurt?" J.L. asked.

"No, no." she said between coughing.

J.L. started picking his way out for both of them but within the moment Caleb and Andy were there pulling away lumber and such to help make their exit easier. Once out and after a minute of catching breaths J.L. asked. "What in tarnation . . . ?"

Caleb just shook his hand, smacked the dust off his clothes and said, "I don't rightly know other than I guess he wasn't going to be taken alive."

"I guess that we could take that as an admission of guilt and maybe some relief to the Thomas family. But Mai Lee is safe so that matters most now."

As the excitement subsided, J.L.'s foot began to remind him that he had an injury. "I think I need to get this boot off and see what damage that ole coot did to my foot."

Caleb helped J.L. get down to the creek supporting him one side while he gingerly stepped on the wounded foot. "I don't think your boot is worth anything, I am going to cut if off" said Andy, who had appointed himself the doctor at the moment. J.L.'s foot had begun to swell. With J.L. sitting on a rock at water's edge, Andy gingerly cut off the boot. There was a three to four inch burned gash along J.L.'s heal and side. He was very happy to dunk it in the cold water. That instantly took away the pain. After a good soaking Mai Lee had made up of bandage of cloth from something she found, wrapped willow leaves and other plants in it and secured it to J.L.'s foot.

"It doesn't look like you oughta be going anywhere today." said Andy.

"It's not bad, give me a bit and if we need to leave today I can do it" answered J.L.

After that they took some time to rest and recoup a little down by the river. Wash up a bit from all the dust and to get a little food and water seemed to do a world of good. And while it seemed like a whole day had gone by it was still quite early – just noon.

As they sat around on rocks by the river, J.L. with his foot propped up, Caleb asked, "Do you think he had a fortune in ore up in the mine?"

"Hard to say, probably some but I suspect if there was some that he had cleaned it would be elsewhere, maybe somewhere in what's left of the shack" Answered J.L.

"We should take a hard look for that for a while, I guess stay here the night. Mai Lee, is that alright with you?" Caleb responded back.

"Yes, yes, I think there something to be found, not know where but we should look" said Mai Lee.

"Well, young lady, if there is, it is yours" said Caleb with J.L. and Andy nodding in approval.

Caleb and Andy looked through the cabin piece by piece while Mai Lee fussed about J.L. He convinced her that he was alright. Then he found a comfortable spot on the ground, his feet elevated, hat pulled down low and was soon asleep.

He only woke when Andy and Caleb returned to the river. They were whooping it up a bit. "Yessirree, Mai Lee, this will never pay you back for all the trouble you and your friends endured but it will help a bit" said Caleb, who produced two small leather pouches nearly filled with gold and silver."

~~~

The next day the four headed out and back up the canyon. Within an hour they were at the site the Chinese miners had been working. What remained of their bodies lay on the beach. The three men buried the remains. Even though he wasn't comfortable with it, J.L. said a prayer. Mai Lee sat on a rock and seemed to be singing some song that seemed appropriate for the somber occasion.

And then it was another long week of riding before Caleb, J.L. and Mai Lee arrived back in The Dalles.

Epilogue

Another month passed by and fall was well in swing. Chang had recovered and he and Mai Lee had found some rooms in town. Both had found some work and were making a new life.

The little girls had now adjusted to their new parents for the most part. Maddie relished the experience and J.L. loved the little girls as if they were his own although he wasn't always sure what to do with them. Jacob liked being a big brother but also liked being back in school and little peace away from them.

On one Saturday, much to J.L.'s surprise Abigail and Benjamin Thomas showed up at their door. They had gotten directions from folks in town. They were responding to a wire that J.L. had sent months ago explaining the latest regarding Joseph's partner and the outcome of that.

After they had settled into talk, Maddie fussing with some refreshment and the children sent outside to play they didn't waste any time to coming to the point of their visit.

"J.L. we have come to ask what your plans are, what are your thoughts about the circuit riding ministry. We have been in much prayer about it and we want to know what you are thinking and how we might assist you." stated Abigail.

"We have been busy what with this new family, the ranch. And I have been doing some blacksmithing and just, you know, what it takes to provide. But I have been giving it a matter of prayer. I know Maddie has too. There is a part of me that just says no way and yet there is something stirring that, well, I don't know how to explain it."

"Perhaps that is the prompting of the Holy Spirit" answered Ben.

"Maybe, but you know I don't really know much about the Bible, the duties, or all of those things. I would be just a babe in the woods or more like a bull in a china shop I suspect." J.L. said with an unexpected snicker in his voice.

"That is what we would like to help you with too. There is some training in Portland that we would like to send you too. It will be a way for you to find out. Meet and learn from people that would help you better decide. Would you be open to that?" Abigail persisted.

"Maybe, I mean sure, um, but I can't imagine it at this time of year."

"We would arrange for you to go in the spring. You would spend a couple of weeks. Maddie could go as well. Would you pray about that?"

"Sure thing, we will. Maddie, what do you think about this?" said J.L. looking at her direct. She had been quiet as a mouse through this discussion.

Maddie said very thoughtfully, "I have been praying much about this – in fact can't seem to get it off my mind. I think we should find out. The Lord has called you, John, that I know just not what."

Tentative plans were then made for spring. But as most of us find out sooner or later, The Lord's ways are higher than ours and our plans are often soon forgotten as we deal with the things at hand.

Soon the rain, the snow and the winds came. And the gorge country became a land of white snow. The wind could be so mean, it seemed, just to stay warm was a big challenge. J.L. and Jacob's main task these days was trying to keep enough fuel for the fireplace and the cook stove, enough hay and grain for the animals and butchered beef, venison and anything else they could hunt to keep this family of five fed.

Christmas seemed extra special this year as there were more presents to get for two little girls and one boy who was becoming a young man. The Christmas Eve service took on a more blessed perspective for Maddie and she reconsidered the Christ child as the two girls snuggled in her lap.

And before you knew it, spring began once again. The white hills turned green, the wild flowers began to shout out in a wild mix of colors.

Also, that spring, came a telegraph for J.L. It was from the Thomas family. It told of a meeting and an appointment in Portland that they would hope J.L. would keep. It was with those devout men and women who carried the Lord's torch to the lost of the Northwest.

J.L. had not forgotten this but it certainly had been put on the back burner. Maddie encouraged, "It is something for you to find out about, J.L. What harm could come out of you just going to Portland?"

They both had no idea how profound that rhetorical question could be.

Dennis Ellingson has served as a pastor and a counselor. He is the author of the first of the Circuit Rider series, "The Painted Hills, the best selling book, "God's Healing Herb" plus "God's Wild Herbs" and along with his wife, Kit, "The Godly Grandparent". Dennis is a born and raised Oregonian who loves to explore God's creation in the Oregon land, East of the Cascades. He and Kit reside in beautiful and scenic Southern Oregon.

All photographs are by Kit Ellingson taken in the Hells Canyon area.